Switch Stance

A CONTEMPORARY SPORTS ROMCOM

A Charitable Endeavors Novel

M.E. CARTER
ANDREA JOHNSTON

Switch Stance:
Riding the opposite direction than usual,
in the opposite stance, and making it look normal.

Switch Stance

A CONTEMPORARY SPORTS ROMCOM

Chapter 1

Aggi

"I love you," he whispers huskily into my ear. "You are the woman I've been dreaming of."

He takes me into his strong, muscular arms and holds me close, his hardening length pressed against my stomach. The feeling makes me gasp with anticipated pleasure.

"I want to make love to you," he breathes, grabbing my hair and pulling my head back so he has access to my neck where he peppers kisses all the way down to my shoulder. I shudder and feel goosebumps cover my exposed flesh.

He's husky and strong and . . . all man.

"Please, please let me be inside you," he pleads. "I want to take you. To make you mine. To mark you from the inside out."

"I want that too," I practically shout, my dreams finally about to come true.

His nostrils flare and he leans down, his arm wrapped under my knees as he pulls me to his chest *and runs up the stairs to his giant master bedroom. I feel like Scarlett O'Hara.*

Throwing me onto the bed, I watch as he strips down to nothing, his nakedness on full display . . . strong, thick, hard, waiting for me.

He stalks over to the bed, his eyes never leaving mine. My belly quivers as I wait for him to strip me of my clothes, waiting for him to love me.

He makes quick work of my pants, then my panties, then he holds me open and leans in, a feral growl coming from deep within as his tongue begins to . . .

A hard shove knocks my thoughts off track. A random stranger of the male variety doesn't seem to notice he just barreled right into the back of my chair, practically knocking my computer bag onto the floor. He just keeps walking.

I suppose it's probably a good thing. My over the top, 80s romance fantasies are not what I'm supposed to be working on right now.

No. I, Agnes Sylvester, known as Adeline Snow to the romance reading community, have work to do and daydreams are not it.

As a New York Times best-selling author, my days are spent spilling my fantasies onto paper for the masses. Usually I do it well. You don't become a best-selling author by writing crap.

Well, most authors don't. As in all industries, there are exceptions to the rule.

I shake my head to rid myself of those thoughts. Rule number one of Author 101 states: "Don't worry about what others are doing. Just write the best story you can."

I actually don't know if there is an Author 101 class. But if there were, that would be rule number one. Because truly, you can't control what others do, only what kind of effort you put in. At least, that's the motto I try to live by. So far, it's worked for me.

Which is part of the reason I need to focus.

I look back into the eyes of my muse, skateboarding god Spencer Garrison, and will a new fantasy to come to life. Usually, staring at a picture of him works. It's why I have several screenshots of his Instagram pictures on my phone. It's why I was able to write two and a half complete novels during the last X Games. It's also why I'm sitting at the bookstore staring at a cardboard cutout of him. To everyone else, he's advertising a new healthy lifestyle book he's releasing soon. To me, he's research.

Unfortunately, it's not working, and I feel myself getting more and more frustrated.

My phone rings scaring the crap out of me. It's my editor, Greer.

Grabbing it, I answer with, "How did you know I was suffering from a horrific case of writer's block? Do you have superpowers?"

She chuckles under her breath. "Are you at the bookstore?"

My eyes widen dramatically. If I do nothing else well in life, being dramatic is my strength. "How did you know that?"

"Are you staring at a cardboard cutout of Spencer?"

Now my jaw drops. "No, really, are you stalking me? Where are you? You're hiding behind one of the bookshelves, aren't you?" I ask as I bend this way and that, looking around the bookstore, aka my latest writing dive.

This time she laughs out loud. I would never tell her, but I like hearing her laugh. She's been my editor since my very first indie book, before I was picked up by my publisher, and she's had a rough few years. She puts on a brave face, but Greer has an ex-husband in prison, a special needs teenager and a teenage daughter. Hearing her happy makes me relax.

"What if I told you I was standing right behind Spencer's cardboard body, staring at you thr.ough the holes in his eyes?"

She's joking. At least I hope she's joking.

"I'd tell you that was the creepiest thing you've ever said, and I may have to end this friendship."

She gasps. "You wouldn't dare."

"No, I wouldn't dare. But I really hope you're not here because that would be weird, and I refuse to be involved if you get arrested for loitering."

"Well, you can relax, my friend. I am not stalking you. I'm sitting in my new office chair in my new office in my new house."

Now my ears perk up. Greer moved to Texas a few weeks ago, and I've been hounding her for pictures of her new place ever since. There's nothing I love more than floor plans and decorating and DIY. "Oooh!

That sounds amazing! Did you get all your books un-packed?" Because of course that is the most important part of any move.

"Sadly, I may not have enough shelving. I may need to get another custom-made one."

I sigh dreamily and close my eyes, resting my head on my fist. "Those are the single greatest words you have ever said to me."

"I knew you'd appreciate it."

"Seriously. I may have just had a Big O right in this bookstore." I grimace when I open my eyes only to see a woman glaring at me, a look of shock on her face as she covers her tween's ears. The kid is grinning like the pervy little twelve-year-old he probably is. "Sorry," I mouth as she walks away, dragging the kid behind her.

"You are making inappropriate comments in pub-lic. Exactly how bad is this block? If you drop the F-bomb, I'm flying out there to put you on a fifty-one-fifty-hold at the local psych ward."

I groan, dreams of custom bookshelves put on the back burner as Greer brings me back to reality. "Please don't. I hear Courtney Love might be back in there, and she frightens me. I don't want to be her bitch."

"Oh my. This is bad."

Shifting in the chair, I get down to business. As much as I'd like to avoid it, I still have a job to do. "I don't know what to do, Greer. I'm really stuck this time."

She immediately moves out of friend mode and into work mode, putting on her encourager cap. "First of all, it's a psych ward, not a prison. No one will make you their bitch."

"You've never been there. You don't know that for sure."

"Second," she interrupts, ignoring my theatrics, "you say that every time, Adeline, and you're never actually stuck. You only need a little motivation."

"Which is why I'm here. I'm getting my motivation."

"Why don't you buy your own cardboard cut-out of Spencer for your house?"

"Because that would be creepy." I bite my lip before admitting to the coffee table book I have opened to his page at home. Some things a girl needs to keep to herself.

"No creepier than sitting in a public store staring at it from across the room."

I drop my head on the table in front of me in defeat and whine, "I don't know what to do, Greer."

"Well, let's sort this out. What do you have so far?"

This right here is why I keep Greer around. I took a chance on her when I wrote my first indie book and trusted her to edit it. Granted, she took a chance on my writing too. When that book randomly became a best seller, I was picked up by a publisher who provided a new editor. It's a nice perk and all, but it's not the same. The editor from my publishing house doesn't help me work through my blocks. She merely approves my drafts or makes me do them again. I never know which one it will be and is likely based on the latest reader poll about what they want. Greer, on the other hand, actually helps me push through my storylines. She brainstorms with me. She helps me figure out my character motivation. And then she goes through it all with a fine-toothed comb, so I know it's the best it can possibly be before it goes to my "real" editor.

Lifting my head up and pushing my dark, unruly hair out of my face, I give her all the details. "He's a surfer."

"Ooooh, surfing this time," she coos. "I like it. You haven't done that one yet. What else?"

"That's it. It's all I have. He's a surfer."

With the way her tone changes, I swear there is a screech of tires somewhere. "Adeline."

"Yes," I say sheepishly.

"Honey, you do know you're supposed to have thirty thousand words to me in the next month."

"I know." I drop my head on the table again. I'm going to have a bruise on my forehead if I keep doing this. "I've never been blocked this badly before. I don't know what's going on. I'm looking at my muse—right at him." The same guy that ran into me before takes this exact moment to look at me, then the cutout, then at me again. I feel my face flame. "Oh crap. I just got caught looking at my muse."

Damn that Greer and her sudden burst of laughter.

"This isn't funny," I whisper harshly. "I can't seem to get any inspiration, and I certainly can't do it when I keep getting caught trying to find it."

"Maybe you need to find a new muse."

A shrill gasp comes from somewhere deep within my soul and makes its way through the phone line. "You take that back," I whisper harshly. She thinks it's funny when I get all theatrical, the jerk.

I love her.

"Okay, okay, fine," she responds, still chuckling. "Spencer is your muse. He will always be your muse. Why not take it a step further?"

I know what she's implying and *is she insane?!*

"I can't write about what he actually does!"

"Adeline Snow" has spent several years writing about sexy, extreme sport athletes. Some would say I have cornered the market on sports romance, although I would say there's room for all authors in that genre.

I have written about snowboarders and cave diving and white-water rafting. I have written about BMX racing and motocrossers and free climbing. I even wrote one book about a roller derby which was awesome to research by the way. I still meet with the captain of our local team for drinks sometimes. She looks like that lady from American Pickers who sends the guys places to pick. I love her.

But I have never and will never write about skateboarding. It's easy to create fantasies based on Spencer Garrison excelling at anything and everything extreme. Because he totally could. I just know it. But to actually write about his sport would be too close to real life for me, and I would be *mortified* if anyone figured out who my muse is. It's bad enough Greer knows.

If our paths were to ever cross, I. Would. Die.

"Well, what about making the heroine a single mom?" Greer tosses out.

I grimace. "Ugh. It's been done."

"What if she's older?"

I crinkle my nose. "Like a cougar story?"

"Yeah. Why not?"

"I'm just not feeling it," I say with a shrug.

"How about a secret baby?"

The gears start turning in my brain and I sit up straight. "Wait. Like he left town to pursue his dream of being a pro surfer, and on his way across the country, he has a one-night stand and doesn't know he has a child until she finally tracks him down?"

"Oh, Adeline that sounds great."

"Eh. Too cliché." I slump down in my chair. I don't want to write what everyone else writes. There are thousands of romance books about football, and soccer, and even bull riding. It's why I focus on Extreme Sports. I've been a fan of the less-than-mainstream sports and have watched the X Games religiously since I was a kid. My best friend, Todd, and I used to dream of one day winning a medal and would grab our skateboards as soon as the games were over to practice on a makeshift ramp we'd made out of an old piece of plywood and some wooden pallets.

We still take Mrs. Chilson Christmas cookies as thanks for the many times she was Todd's ER nurse when he broke his arm.

"You really are blocked." It's like she thinks my theatrics are all for naught. I may be over the top, but I'm always honest when I do it.

"I am, Greer. I so am." I breathe a heavy sigh. "Maybe I need to go on this promotional tour and meet some people to inspire me. You know how much wandering around new cities and taking pictures helps open up my brain to creativity."

"That'll probably help."

I make a mental note to pack the new camera I splurged on when I received my last signing bonus. I love playing tourist. But not just any tourist. I want to sightsee the places most people never know are there. You'd never find me darkening the door of Carlos & Charlie's in Cancun. But you would see me spending hours walking through the ruins of Tulum.

We chat for a few more minutes about my work-not-actually-in-progress as well as a few more administrative things before her workday ends and her mom-day begins.

"Hey, Adi, I need to let you go. Kids are getting out of school, and I need to get into mom mode. They've only been in school for a week so we're trying to get this new routine down."

Poor Greer. I admire her strength. She has so much on her plate, and she pretends to balance it so well. I don't tell her I know she struggles with her own motivation. She would hate that. Instead, I try to be her friend and adjust to her schedule any way I can.

"All right," I respond, glancing back up to my

muse, wishing he would magically give me a story. "Well, wish me luck."

"Good luck. But, Adi, you've got this. I know you do."

I smile because it's nice to know she accommodates me as much as I do her. "Thanks. And hey, Greer?"

"Yeah?"

"You got this too. This move is the best thing for you."

I can practically hear the tears in her eyes. Sometimes she just needs to know I recognize her too.

"Thanks, Adeline. I think we're finally where we're supposed to be."

We hang up and I spend the next few minutes saying a silent prayer for my good friend to meet someone amazing, who loves her for everything she is and loves her children too.

Maybe someday I'll write a book about her. Her story could be very interesting. I jot it down in my plotting notebook. It has several story ideas I've come up with over the years. Sadly, none of them are calling to me right now.

I sigh heavily and look into the vacant eyes of Spencer Garrison. "Come on, Spence. You gotta give me something."

"What?"

I turn to see that same guy sitting next to me now, wondering who I'm talking to. Seriously, where does he keep coming from?

"Uh, nothing." I know my face is flaming red. It's one of the joys of having lily white skin. "Just talking to myself."

He cocks an eyebrow like I'm a weirdo, which admittedly I probably am, and turns away.

That was a close call. I need to keep my talks to Photograph Spencer limited to times when I'm in the safety of my own apartment. Not that it's doing any good these days. I have got to snap out of this writer's block. I just wish I could figure out how.

Chapter 2

Spencer

The genius who designed airplane seats and I need to have a sit-down. A meeting. A *conversation*. These seats were not engineered for anyone over five feet, let alone a six–foot-four man. This is why I try to fly first class whenever possible. Not because I want the free drinks or the hot towels, but because there is at least six inches more of leg room. On the rare occasion, like this one, that I have to fly coach, I'm usually able to sweet talk a flight attendant into a row without someone assigned to the middle seat. I wasn't lucky this time and here I sit, row thirty-seven of forty and the middle seat. Someone kill me now. I'm practically sitting in a fetal position. It's like I've returned to the womb, only without the comfort of white noise and sleep.

After I picked up my first sponsor and began flying regularly, I had one request of whoever made my plane reservations: window seat. I was a kid and loved looking out the window at the bright lights, imagining all the places I would skate. Okay, all the places I planned to skate. Most of the locations on my list included vacant lots, deserted business parks, and other public lo-cations with large signs that read "Keep Out" or "No Skating." It's cute how people think a sign will keep a skater off their property.

As a teenager after a few growth spurts, I moved that preferred seat to the aisle. In the aisle, I can stretch my legs between the flight attendants rolling their carts by and avoid the leg cramps from hell. By the time I turned pro and was pulling in real sponsorship money, I'd upgraded to first class and which seat I was as-signed wasn't an issue. Even now, as I stare down my retirement as a professional skateboarder and X Games medalist, that's how I prefer to fly.

But then there are the random occasions I'm re-sponsible for booking my own flights and forget to actually purchase the ticket until the day before I'm scheduled to leave. Then I end up in the middle seat between Gladys and Martin, playing go between dur-ing the first fight of their vacation. Because of their spat, they refused to switch seats with me. Something about refusing to share an arm rest with someone who can't respect personal boundaries. I'm not thrilled about the role of mediator, but I have to say, I'm with Gladys on this one. Martin really shouldn't eat dairy when he flies.

Thankfully, the captain has announced our descent and my torture is almost over. Or just beginning. I sup-pose it depends on which way you look at it. When I told my sister, Kate, I would do anything she wanted for her thirtieth birthday, I expected her to ask for a weekend at an all-inclusive resort, complete with massages by a hunky guy named Rico and unlimited glasses of rosé. I was wrong. So very, very wrong. No, my smart, over-worked sister, who spends her days working with troubled teens and her nights being a wife and mom, did not choose the all-inclusive resort. She also didn't take up my offer for a weekend in New York, shopping and seeing a Broadway show. Kate also put the kibosh on the offer to watch her children, so she and her husband could take a romantic getaway to a cabin in the woods.

What did she choose for her amazing birthday celebration?

A convention. Not just any convention, a romance book convention. I have absolutely no idea what the weekend will entail. All I know is she was over the moon excited when I bought her the VIP tickets and booked a hotel room for her and her best friend. But, joke was on me when she opened her card with the itinerary printed. She peered up at me with her big doe eyes, bottom lip stuck out like it was injured, and mock sniffled when she asked me to go with her instead of a girlfriend. Me. Spencer Garrison, five-time X Games gold medalist, professional skateboarder, and not a woman. Or a man who reads romance, because I'm assuming there are some of those out there. I don't judge them for it. They're allowed to be in touch with their feelings or whatever.

But Kate is my sister, and I love her more than anyone else in this world, which she knows and uses to her advantage. So, here I am, in the middle seat of an airplane wishing Martin had said no to the cheese board and praying my sister remembers this weekend for the rest of her life because it's the last gift I'm ever giving her.

•••

"Freddy, I hear what you're saying but no."

With a heavy sigh, my agent grumbles under his breath before trying again to convince me to change my stance on promotional tours. "Spencer, you have to see the benefit of this tour from a business perspective. You've been dropping hints about potential retirement, and while I think you're an idiot for even considering that, the damage may be done. We need to get ahead of this and get you out there, show your sponsors your commitment."

"No." My response is louder than I planned and the other passengers disembarking from the plane look at me with wide eyes. Mouthing "sorry," I tug my backpack higher on my shoulder as I smile to the flight attendants on my way out.

The minute we landed I, like most of the passengers, pulled my cell from the seat pouch in front of me and powered it up. My plan was to text Kate and let her know I landed and would meet her outside. Instead, I was greeted with an overwhelming amount of notifications. Not only were there a few voice messages but also half a dozen texts from my agent. I planned to ignore the messages from Freddy until I was at the hotel, showered, and had a cold beer in my hand. Lately, most conversations with Freddy require a beer. He's been up my ass about my plans to retire, and I knew this wouldn't be any different. After pulling my carryon from the overhead bin, I wait patiently for the other passengers to disembark as Gladys tries to pull me back into their conversation. Slightly rude but mostly in desperation, I click the call button on Freddy's name as I excuse myself from Gladys. Even Freddy's harassment is better than having to endure Martin's puppy dog eyes when I side against him.

"It'll be great exposure for the foundation." Freddy's voice isn't smug like it should be. He knows he has me by the balls now. My foundation. The greatest achievement to come from this career of mine.

"I'll think about it. But for now, I'm going to spend the weekend with my sister. Family first, Fred. Speaking of, don't you have like an anniversary or birthday thing today?"

"Shit. I didn't even realize the time. I'll call you tomorrow so we can talk about this more."

The line goes dead and I'm relieved. For the first time, remembering my agent's wedding anniversary came in handy. But how could I forget? Last year, he almost ended up on my couch for forgetting and getting home three hours late. Apparently the wifey had made a special dinner and fell asleep wearing a negligee for the occasion. For the guy who tries to organize my life, he doesn't do such a great job of taking care of his own.

My walk through the airport is quick, but since I was distracted by Freddy I failed to text Kate. Great.

Me: Landed. I'm heading out now. No luggage.

Kate: I just got the stink eye from Security. Looping

around. Be about ten.

Me: NO TEXTING AND DRIVING!

Kate: Voice to text ducker!

Kate: Ducker!

Kate: Forget it. I'll call you it when I see you. Ten.

I love my sister and considering her potty mouth, I'm sure the "d" in ducker is supposed to be an "f." Since I have a few minutes, I swing by the bathroom to handle business before continuing my walk to the pick-up spots at the curb. When my phone rings, I assume it's either my sister or Freddy, so I answer with a fake accent.

"Nico's Pizza what's ya pleasure?"

"Yes, I'm looking for Spencer Garrison?"

Shit, that's not Kate nor Freddy. Clearing my throat, I say, "Speaking."

"Mr. Garrison, this is Officer Hertz with the Lexington Police Department."

The Lexington PD? I just finished building my house in Lexington and have only spent a few weeks there. What could the police be calling me about? Shit, I hope there wasn't a fire or something. That would be just my luck. To build an amazing home on acreage only to have it burn to the ground before I can even enjoy it. Before I can host my family there. Before I can show my mom and my sister what all the broken bones, missed holidays, and work has been for.

"What can I do for you, Officer?"

"Sir, I'm calling about a break-in at your home."

"A break-in? I suppose the thieves were disappointed with the lack of items to steal." My laugh is not returned so I clear my throat before continuing. "How was it broken into? I have a great security system, and it isn't like the house is easily accessible."

"Well, it appears a bunch of teenagers helped themselves to your pool and skate setup. They didn't actually make it in the house."

This is why I started my foundation. I know firsthand teenagers with a lot of time on their hands have too many opportunities to make poor life choices. Choices that will follow them for the rest of their lives, taint their history. The Garrison Foundation's primary objective is work with communities to build alternative recreation opportunities for kids. Of course, I'd like a skate park in every city across the nation, but that isn't always feasible. Instead, my team works with community leaders to help fund and create programs that fit each city.

"Was anyone injured?"

"No, sir. And, unfortunately, we were only able to apprehend two of the kids. The rest fled."

"They left two behind? That sucks for them," I say as I step out through the sliding doors of the airport and into the warm Chicago night. Late summer is definitely in the air here in Illinois. It's nowhere near the pits of hell also known as a late Texas summer, like the kind I grew up in. I'm grateful for that.

"Yeah it does. Look, normally we'd write the kids up, but these two . . ." He pauses, and I hear a door close before he continues. "Look, Mr. Garrison, I don't think these two boys intended to do any harm. They're good kids, one just moved to town with his mom, and I think he was just trying to look cool to the older kids. He even had your gate code."

He had my gate code? Who could have had my gate code? I wrack my brain thinking about that when it dawns on me . . . Landon. I bet this is the kid working with Landon and helping him deliver the custom furniture he's building for the house. Dammit.

"Look Officer Hertz, I don't want to be the reason these kids have a blemish on their record. How about you . . . can you hold on for a sec?" I ask when I spot Kate's minivan approaching before she cuts off a few cars and pulls to the curb. I roll my eyes. Chances are when I open this door she'll be playing some awful pop music that will make my ears bleed and start shouting the correct word her voice to text didn't catch.

I point to my phone indicating I'm actually talking to someone before I open the door and she nods in response before reaching for the radio dial. When I'm sure the music is turned down and she won't embarrass me too much, I open the passenger door and toss my bag in as I continue my call.

"Sorry about that. I think I know one of these kids, well his mom and her boyfriend anyway. I don't want to press charges or anything. But," I say as Kate shoots a wide-eyed look at me. Shaking my head to let her know it's not a big deal, I continue, "What do you think about scaring these kids a little and letting them know the next time they may not be so lucky?"

"I like the way you think, Mr. Garrison. Consider

it done. I'll call you later to let you know how it goes."

"Sounds good. Thank you for calling."

I disconnect the call and look to my sister who is chewing on her bottom lip. I know it's killing her not to speak.

"Proceed, sister."

"Fucker. That's what I was calling you. My damn phone is an idiot."

Laughing, I pat her shoulder and laugh. "Your phone?"

Sighing she says, "Fine, not my phone. Me. I wasn't circling. I was getting coffee. I got you something so don't be mad." I look to where she's pointing and smile when I see a large coffee and a pastry. "But I was also calling you a fucker. Whew," she says with an exaggerated exhale. "That's better. Now why were you not pressing charges?"

"It's a long story. I'll tell you over a burger and a beer. Which, there will be a lot of if I'm doing this weekend with you."

My sister doesn't respond and instead turns the dial on the radio as one of my favorite Pennywise songs pumps through the speakers. Surprised, I look to my sister who has a huge smile on her face.

"It's the least I can do if you're going to spend all weekend lugging my books around and being my personal photographer."

Great. If she's buttering me up with music this is really going to be a long weekend.

"I wish you would have taken me up on my offer to buy you a plane ticket. I can't believe you drove." I have hated the idea of her being alone on the road for hours on end.

"Oh stop. This is like a vacation. I have three children, Spencer. I barely pee without an audience. Hours in the car alone is like a vacation."

Settling into my seat, I wonder what I've gotten myself into.

Chapter 3

Aggi

I have never considered myself a people person.

Don't get me wrong, I'm not anti-people. I like personalities and character traits and quirks. I like stories of the underdog overcoming. I like the history our great-great-gran-whatevers tell.

But the idea of going to a concert or dinner party has always made me nearly hyperventilate. I'm likely to say something really weird like responding to someone's "Hi" with "Thank you." It's easier to stick to myself and a couple of people who are either as odd as me or don't have a judgy bone in their body.

That's one of the reasons I like my job so much. My favorite part is creating stories, of course. But as an added bonus, I don't have to sit in an office and interact with people who are overworked, underpaid, and badly need a shot of caffeine. Plus, the age of social media means I get to connect with people who are very like-minded.

Readers may not agree on everything, but we all love the written word. I learned at the beginning of my career, as long as I talk about the latest book I read, I'm going to connect with someone despite my ineptness. Especially online.

But today isn't online. Today is live and in person. So, seeing the long line of readers waiting to get into today's signing has me full of anxiety. Some of them have been here for hours with their empty carts waiting to be filled with books by their favorite authors. Many of them gave up standing long ago and are sitting on the floor.

Wait . . . did someone . . .?

Yep. Someone brought her own collapsible chair to sit in while she waits.

That is hard core and a lot of pressure to live up to. Which is funny because I don't have to impress them. For some strange reason I still haven't figured out, they're here for my books. My novels speak for themselves and, thankfully, that puts me one step ahead of the social niceties. To make it even easier, at one time Greer made me memorize a list of topic questions I can ask while signing a book. Things like, "Are you having a good time?" and "Where did you come in from?" You know, easy conversation starters that always gets someone talking.

Well, almost always. There was that one time a young girl froze. When I asked where she drove in from, she said, "My car." Poor girl turned red as a tomato until I told her I once accidentally kissed my pastor on the lips when he went in for my cheek. She giggled so loudly she snorted and turned red again. Hey I tried. But the socially awkward really shouldn't lead the socially awkward. It's in the nerd girl handbook or something.

Walking past the line of readers, I keep my head down, hoping not to be noticed yet. I still need to mentally prepare myself for the five hundred plus people here for the events. That's plural.

Five hundred? Don't think about it, Aggi. Maybe I can leave the signing early and claim I'm behind on my deadline. It's not a lie. I'm way behind.

I roll my eyes at myself because there's no way I'll be leaving early. "Adeline Snow" has already been placed in one of the coveted corner spots to accommodate the anticipated line. No pressure there.

The crowd suddenly gets excited and I make the mistake of looking up to see what's happening. That's when I realize they're looking at me.

"Ohmygod, it's Adeline Snow!" someone yells and people begin cheering.

This is the part that always gets me. What am I supposed to do when people are screaming for me? Wave? Take a bow? Shake hands and kiss babies? No one has trained me for this kind of attention.

So, I do the only thing I can think of . . . I awkwardly curtsy, stumbling as I trip over my own high heel. Racing to the closed door that will get me into the banquet hall, and hopefully to safety, I pray I won't trip again. I love wearing heels to these events. It's the only time I dress up, and combined with my favorite '50s-inspired red satin dress and coifed hair, it seems to go well with the brand my publicist and I created, but they are not conducive to running from a crowd.

Swinging the door open, I step inside and pull it shut behind me. Holding my hand over my chest, I lean against the door and will my breathing to slow down. I should be used to this by now. It's not like it's my first event.

"I don't know why you are always so surprised when the readers are excited to see you."

Opening my eyes, I see my friend Sharon pulling paper wristbands apart in preparation for today. Sharon is at all the big events. She's like the volunteer extraordinaire—always willing to help. Always with a smile on her face. She gets there early and stays late. Plus, she's always kind, no matter how freaked out you may be.

"I never seem to learn, do I?" I joke back.

She giggles. "Not ever. You know what else you never learn?"

Suddenly, I'm falling backward and landing on my rear in the hall where everyone can see me.

"Oh! I'm so sorry! I didn't know you were standing there!" I look up to see Donna Moreno, best-selling erotica romance author and practically a model, standing over me.

Climbing to my feet, Sharon is by my side almost instantaneously to help me get my bearings straight again. "You never learn not to lean against the doors of the banquet halls. That's what, twice you've fallen on your rear when the door swings open?"

"Three times," I admit, my face turning red once

again. And not a nice shade. No, my face gets all splotchy red, like I've been slapped several times over. "You weren't in Atlanta a few weeks ago."

Sharon giggles and points out it wasn't the only mistake I've made in the last few seconds. "You do realize you came in through the wrong door, right?" No, no I didn't. "Don't worry, I'll take you the back way, so you don't have to walk past the crowd again."

Donna takes her arm in mine and walks with me to the stage where the panels are getting ready to begin. "Seriously, Adeline, I'm so sorry. You aren't hurt, are you?"

"Just embarrassed. But that's nothing unusual for me," I joke, making her laugh a deep, sexy laugh.

I've always liked Donna. She's the total package. Like Miss America package. With long, thick blond hair, and perfect features, you might expect to see her on the big screen. Or at least a Pantene commercial. But no. She's a former attorney who now writes erotic romance full time. And she's one of the nicest people I know. She charms the pants off readers and publishers alike. That's actually how we met—when my publisher picked her up. If there was ever a person I would pick to open a door and humiliate me in front of all our fans, it's my girl crush.

We step up on the stage that's overlooking a few dozen chairs. There are only two water bottles sitting on the long table. Drat. That means it's only the two of us. I was hoping there would be four people answering questions. It's easier to fade into the background.

"Are you excited about today?" she asks me kindly, while I accidentally dribble some water down my chin because curtsying, standing, *and* drinking seem to have eluded me. I better stay away from stairs today. And balconies. The observation deck on the Hancock Building . . .

Wiping my dress off with my hand, I respond, "You know I don't care for panels. I always freeze up."

She pats my arm. And not from condescension. No, she's genuine and warm and truly concerned about my well-being. "Adeline, you need to have more confidence in yourself and your abilities. Your stories are amazing. That's why the readers want to be here. They want to hear what you have to say."

I find myself looking into her eyes a few seconds too long, mesmerized by the green color. This would be a really strange moment if she wasn't used to my quirky behavior.

Finally, I snap out of it. "I'm not sure I have much to give them these days." I sigh. "I really should be in my room writing. Maybe you could do the panel by yourself?" I raise my eyebrows as the idea takes on some merit. "Oh! That's actually a good idea! I'm about twenty thousand words behind and getting further off my deadline every day. I could spend the next hour writing and . . ."

I look up and see Donna shaking her head.

"You don't think that's a good idea, do you?"

"No, I don't. Come on, Adeline. We all have creative blocks. It's part of being an author. But you'll pull through it. You probably just need to meet someone new, find a muse to get you out of your funk. The best place to do that is at an event like this where it's packed with people."

That reminder is not helping me want to stay. But I suppose she's right. Besides, the doors are open, and people are making their way to their seats. There's no way I'd be able to gracefully exit with my track record so far. It's probably best to stay sitting down.

Donna and I continue to chat for a few more minutes. Actually, Donna chats and I do my best to respond appropriately. She's always going on mission trips with her church, which I find to be a bit ironic since she writes erotica. Then again, I write about extreme sports and almost fell wearing high heels, so I don't judge her choices. I just find the juxtaposition so interesting.

Plus, she's interesting. On this last trip, she helped dig a well in an Ethiopian village. I love to travel and all, but I can honestly say it has never crossed my mind to go to Ethiopia. Or dig a well.

Just one more reason Donna should be wearing a crown.

After the flurry of chaos when the readers began filling the room, everyone is seated, and Sharon greets our guests. The excitement is practically palpable. Everyone is so excited to be here. Well, except one guy who is staring at his phone. I could be frustrated by his lack of interest, but I'm not. I always appreciate the men who show up for these events. A few of them are readers, but by far, most of the men I meet are husbands and boyfriends who come to be an extra set of hands for someone they love. That is way sexier than any book boyfriend I've ever read, because it's genuine sacrifice. Well, except for any book boyfriend modeled after Spencer Garrison because he's perfect and no one will ever tell me otherwise.

"Donna and Adeline are here to talk to you today about character development," Sharon says, and my ears perk up.

I admit I didn't look at the topic of discussion because I usually do the least amount of talking I can, so this is surprising, and a little concerning, to say the least.

"Ladies"—Sharon turns to address us directly even though she's still holding the microphone—"the floor is yours."

As Sharon steps off the stage and disappears into the adjoining room where the signing will be held, everyone claps. Once the noise dies down, I turn to Donna to take the lead. There is no way I can do much with a topic like this. My character development is easy . . .

Think of Spencer.

Boom. Done.

Yes, yes, I know there is more to it, but that's where it always begins and ends for me. No way am I telling a crowd of people that information.

Donna, of course, doesn't skip a beat. "Good morning everyone," her deep, raspy voice says into the microphone. If this author thing doesn't work out, she needs to be a narrator. "Character development can make or break a story. You can have the best plot lines, the best twists, the best writing, but if your characters are boring, none of the good stuff will make a difference. One of the things I do with every book is write a sort of résumé for every character. Their name, age, where they're from. Who their family is and any important experiences they may have had in their life. I even put their favorite kind of coffee because you can tell a lot by how a person takes their coffee."

I furrow my brow slightly thinking about that statement. Is it true? Can you tell how a person will respond to a situation by their morning joe? And if so, what does Spencer drink?

Shaking my head like I'm clearing out my brain, I try to focus back on Donna, who is now talking about how she organizes all those character résumés.

Seriously, is there anything she can't do? I bet she's an interior decorator or feng shui expert on the side.

I should get her to look at my apartment. Maybe rearranging my furniture will let my energy flow better so I can figure out this next storyline. I could get a plant, maybe one of those weird sparkly balls people put in their garden. Would that work in my living room? I should check on that . . .

A change in energy of the room has me looking up only to realize it wasn't a change in energy. It was silence. Donna is done talking and now everyone is staring at me, waiting for me to say something.

I feel my face heat up and I try not to flash my wide-eyed hysterical look, so I do the only thing I can think of. I grab the microphone in front of me and say, "I agree with everything Donna said."

The crowd laughs, so I assume that was a good enough answer. Truly, if they've been to any event I've been to before or have heard any of my interviews, they should already know I'm woefully ill-prepared to be the center of attention.

Fortunately, the years of debate training has my colleague fully prepared to ad lib. "Why don't we open the floor to questions. Yes," she says, pointing to someone in the crowd. "You in the blue shirt."

A woman stands up a little too quickly and her chairs makes a screeching sound as it slides across the floor. She's wearing jeans and a "Team Extreme" T-shirt. I smile because she must be from my reader group, which means I might know her name. It's always fun to meet someone I've interacted with. "I'm so excited to be here and meet you two." She's practically bouncing on her toes. I like her already. "First I want to make sure Adeline is okay from her fall in the hallway."

I don't like her as much anymore.

Everyone laughs, myself included, even though it feels forced. "I fall down all the time," I say truthfully. "I barely noticed."

It's not really a funny answer, but apparently it satisfies her because she laughs before asking something else.

"Oh good. Okay." She sounds out of breath and part of me wonders if she's going to pass out from not breathing enough. "Um, my real question is, who is your muse, Adeline?"

My thoughts come to another screeching halt. Why do people always ask this question? Can't a writer just have great characters in their head that aren't inspired by real people?

I mean, obviously I can't, but can't other authors?

The gerbils in my brain decide to take a break at this exact moment instead of running on their wheel because I can't for the life of me figure out a work-around to this answer.

Come on, gerbils! Don't let me down! Run for your lives! I don't like lying to my readers.

The pause for me to answer turns awkwardly long so I finally give up and leave the truth behind when I say "I don't really have one. I just write the voices in my head."

Okay, not a total lie.

Okay, yes. A total lie. But what else am I supposed to say? The alternative is too private. I don't need people to know I've had a secret fantasy life with Spencer Garrison for years. I know my agent. She would take that information and use it for some giant marketing campaign. And the last thing I need is for Spencer himself to find out that information.

The thought of even accidentally meeting my muse makes me shudder. I don't need that kind of stress in my life. Not in the future and certainly not when I'm on a major deadline.

Chapter 4

Five fifteen in the morning. That's what time Kate's phone started blaring some awful top forty pop song. I have no idea what the words were but there was a lot of "ohhh yeah" and "baby baby" filling our hotel room. I've never claimed to be a morning person, but today I'm taking that to an all new level.

After dinner and a few beers, we wandered the streets of Chicago, playing catch up. And by catching up, I mean we stopped at a few pubs and bars along our walk back to the hotel and by the time I crawled under the covers of my bed, it was well past midnight.

While I rubbed the sleep from my eyes and tried to figure out if the alarm was a mistake, Kate jumped from the bed like it was Christmas morning and she was an excited toddler. After an hour in the bathroom, she emerged ready to start her day. I, on the other hand, was pissy from being woken up early a second time in one hour's time and was planning my revenge for the loss of sleep. But, regardless, I sucked it up, got my ass in the shower, and here we stand in line with hundreds of women waiting for this book thing to start. The waiting alone is hell on my bum knee, which doesn't help my mood.

Taking a sip of my coffee, I try focusing on the conversations around us, talk about the event and who they're most excited to meet instead of the throb running down my leg. One name is said more than others and it has me intrigued to say the least.

"So, do you read this Adeline Snow woman too?"

At the mention of the author's name, Kate flips around to face me, the stacks of books nestled in her rolling cart seemingly forgotten. Eyes wide, her mouth opens and closes like a smallmouth bass, and I chuckle in response.

"Spencer, she's the entire reason we're here. Well," she says, rolling her eyes, "not the *entire* reason but the primary. She's my favorite sports romance author."

"Sports romance? What the hell is that?"

Gasps all around us fill the dead air and I swallow slowly. I think I just committed a major faux pas or there's a male model standing behind me. Who knew that was even a thing? Male models. At romance book events.

"Ladies, I apologize for my brother." Kate's apology is sincere, which I find humorous in itself, but the look on everyone's face around me has me shaking as I hold back the laughter begging to be let out. "Spencer, sports romance is a category within romance. Sports romance, paranormal romance, romantic suspense, and so on. They're all sub-genres within the larger romance genre itself. But Adeline Snow doesn't just write sports romance, she writes *extreme sports romance.*"

"Wait!" one of the women shouts as she pushes Kate to the side and steps in front of me. "Are you Spencer *Garrison*? X Games gold medalist and more importantly, underwear model?"

Dammit to hell. I am going to kill Kate.

"Nope. I get that all the time. We all have that one celebrity look alike, right? I mean, for a few minutes I thought you were Jennifer Lawrence." The woman who is about fifty years old and looks less like Jennifer Lawrence than her mother smiles broadly and turns to her friends giggling. Crisis averted.

"On that note, I'm going to find a place to sit. I can't believe you're going to stand in this line for another hour before this thing starts."

Waving me off as if my discomfort standing here isn't worth her time, Kate turns her attention back to her cart and the women in line. With my coffee in one hand and my phone in another, I walk toward a door I saw a line of women enter. It's closed now but maybe I can sneak in quietly and find a chair to rest. I'm only a few months post-op knee surgery and standing for long periods of time isn't as easy as it used to be.

As I approach the door, a short woman with shoulder length brown hair organizing a pile of fabric shopping style bags spots me and stares at me questioningly. I pause briefly before reaching for the handle to open the door. The move is hers, if she calls me out on entering the room without a ticket I'll give up my quest for a chair. For the first time today, luck is on my side as she smiles and nods her head once.

"Are you one of the models on the panel?"

I probably shouldn't but my knee is killing me, so I decide to roll with it. "Uhh . . . yes. Yes I am."

Waving her hand, she smiles sweetly. "Go on in. They're just about to start," she says before turning her attention back to the bags.

I suppose the modeling I've done for my sponsors has more perks than I realized. Pulling the door open, I quietly enter the room. Approximately two dozen rows of chairs fill the space facing a single table with two women sitting at it. This must be one of the panels Kate told me about. When I purchased the VIP tickets, I assumed it would get her to the front of any line or some sort of special swag bag. From what she explained last night, the swag is a given, but the VIP package includes admission to some panels the authors will be speaking at. I have no idea why she didn't pick this one, but I don't really care as long as I have a place to sit.

The two women, authors I assume, talk among themselves with a third woman holding a microphone. I scan the room for an available seat or a stack of chairs I can pull one from to sit in the back. Unfortunately for me, the only available seat is in the middle of one of the rows between two older women, probably closer to my mom's age than Kate's. When the woman holding the microphone begins to speak, I quickly rush to the empty seat and settle in. The relief on my knee is immediate, and I hope the break will help get me through the day without having to strap on the annoying knee brace I'm supposed to wear.

Setting my coffee on the floor next to my foot, I pull up my phone and tap out a text message to my friend Landon. We exchanged a few texts last night following the debacle with the Lexington PD and the kids who broke into my property. Landon was beyond apologetic and offered to refund the money I paid him for the custom furniture. We're currently negotiating a compromise to his offer. I've raised his demand to refund at least fifty percent to him buying me a bottle of whiskey. My fingers move at rapid pace when I agree to him refunding me ten percent of the cost of the dining room table but only if he'll add on a new entertainment center to my order. His reply is full of colorful language and I chuckle quietly, trying not to draw attention to myself.

What Landon forgets is I used to be that gangly, awkward teenage boy who would have done anything to make friends whenever I moved. If I'd known my favorite skateboarder lived in the same town as me, you damn well better believe I would have figured out a way to break into his personal training site, so of course I'm not as mad as everyone thinks I should be. In fact, I'm almost surprised it took as long as it did for anyone to catch wind of my new setup. Lexington is a small town. Gossip usually happens faster than it did in this case.

I'm pulled from my thoughts as I hear the woman with the microphone introduce the authors who will be speaking. Adeline Snow, my sister's favorite author. And because I'm a loving little brother, I lift my phone, snap a picture of Ms. Snow and shoot it off to Kate.

Kate: ARE YOU KIDDING ME?

Me: Guess those VIP tickets were worth it after all.

I laugh loudly, which I cover with a cough when I see her response is about ten middle finger emojis. Settling into my seat, I look at the woman speaking. I think her name is Diane or Donna, something like that. She's talking about characters and something else I don't hear. I don't hear her because I'm distracted by the pretty woman to her left. With a throwback hairstyle and bright red lips, she's obviously uncomfortable but is doing her best to pretend otherwise. She's not classically beautiful but there's something about her that intrigues me. When it's her turn to speak, I sit up a little straighter and offer my attention.

•••

"I cannot believe you sat only a few feet away from Adeline Snow! I swear you're the luckiest bastard ever."

While I was resting my knee and listening to women ask about muses and character development, my sister was making friends in line. Each of her new friends stand before me, arms crossed over their chest, disapproving looks on their face, as they wait for me to respond. But I know my sister, and I know she isn't done with her mini rant over my luck and her misfortune.

"I mean, you don't even *read!*"

"Whoa there, turbo. I read."

"Sports magazines and the comments on your social media don't count."

"You know I don't follow social media. I hate that crap. What are you all fired up about anyway? It isn't like I met the woman. I just sat there and played games on my phone while I let my knee rest."

Huffing, Kate turns her attention back to her friends, muttering something about last minute additions to her game plan and a color-coded map. I ignore her rant while I begin rummaging through her bag of tricks for a water. Dear Lord, what does she have in here? Three granola bars, a bag of beef jerky, two candy bars, and four waters. What is this, a camping trip? Grabbing one of the waters, I twist the cap and just as I'm about to take my first swig from the bottle, I see the door swing open from the room where the panel was held. Out walks the woman who had emceed the talk, followed by the two authors. Some of the people in line begin to murmur as the authors walk down the hall.

I attempt to grab my sister's attention while taking a drink of water by nudging her with my foot. Her response is a kick to my shins. My response to that is a mumbled "fuck" before I decide to screw with her.

"Excuse me," I say, stepping out of line and toward the authors. The blonde who did most of the talking stops and smiles my way. I've seen that smile before; it's flirtatious and inviting. Normally, I'd flirt back but it isn't her who has my attention.

"Hello to you. Tell me who you're sitting with today, handsome. We need to talk about my upcoming series. I think you'd be perfect for the cover."

"Sorry, I'm not a model," I reply before turning my attention to the woman in red to her left. "You're Adeline Snow, correct?"

The woman stares at me, eyes wide, but no sounds leaving her mouth. No, the only sounds around us are those of my sister repeating "ohmygodohmygod" over and over.

"I'm Spencer. I was in your panel and wanted to tell you I'm looking forward to visiting your table with my sister, Kate. She's a *huge* fan. You should probably watch out for her; she's a little crazy."

I didn't think it was possible for Adeline's eyes to go wider but they do, right before she lets out a long deep breath that sounds like a balloon deflating. Squeaks and all.

Chapter 5

Aggi

This isn't happening. THIS ISN'T HAPPENING!

I cannot be standing in front of Spencer Garrison, gold medal winner, skateboarding legend and every book boyfriend I've created.

Who did I piss off for this to happen? This is what I get for using the last of someone else's parking meter last month, isn't it?

Is it because I saw a penny and didn't pick it up, so I won't have good luck?

There's really no God is there? It's just Zeus and, and . . . those other ones, and I've been smitted. Smitten? Smoten? Smote? Whatever.

Regardless, this is bad. This is so bad.

And now seconds, no hours have gone by while I stand here, frozen and sounding like a deflating balloon. Because that's the sexy kind of impression I want to make when meeting the man I never wanted to lay eyes on for real.

How could this get any worse?

Donna nudges me with her elbow. "Adeline, the man is speaking to you."

That's how. That's how this could get worse. By making a fool out of myself in front of an entire hallway full of readers.

READERS!

Oh geez. Okay, breathe Aggi. Breathe. He's just a man. A hot, talented, smart, amazing man who smells so good. Ohmygod he smells good, I just want to lick him . . .

FOCUS Aggi!

Do not lean in. Pretend he is the hairy barista at your favorite coffee shop. Look up slowly . . .

Nope. Definitely not the hairy barista. Let's try this again. Close your mouth, relax your eyes, deep breath, now speak . . .

"I write books," I blurt out. Spencer looks at me like I'm a freak of nature because obviously I am. Fortunately, Donna is there to save the day.

"He knows that, honey." She grabs my arm lightly and turns back to Spencer, laughing like I'm the funniest thing she's ever heard. "That's our Adeline. Always making jokes for the readers. Aren't you, Adi?"

No. I never even attempt jokes. Just conversation is bad enough. But I can't think, and in this moment, I'll grasp onto anything Donna has to say as long as she gets me out of here quickly.

"Yes."

Spencer furrows his brow, and all I want to do

is summon Dr. Strange to come bend time, so I never leave that panel room and end up here. Because THAT'S not a totally weird and dorky thought at all.

"Okay, um . . ." Spencer clears his throat, obviously uncomfortable now. "I'm gonna, uh, go back to my sister." He gestures over his shoulder and begins moving that way.

"Okay, BYE!" I accidentally yell and wave like an idiot, then turn on my heel as quickly as possible and speed walk away, not looking behind me.

Why is this happening? How is this happening? Why is Spencer Garrison of all people here at a signing?

I barely register the sound of footsteps following me, but I hear her voice. "Adi." It's Donna. She's practically chasing me, yet another strange thing because Donna doesn't run. At least, not in heels. Probably on a treadmill or in a marathon or something. She looks very muscular and fit and *what am even thinking about right now?*

"Adi, slow down." She reaches me and grabs my arm, steering me away from the front door of the hotel which is my path to freedom from my worst nightmare come to life, and straight into the restaurant and a back table.

Guiding me to a table by the window, she plunks down in the chair across from me and spouts off some sort of instructions to the waitstaff. I can barely hear her as I sit with my elbows on the table, face in my hands.

Suddenly, a glass of water is placed in front of me. "Drink." Donna's demanding tone has me looking up at her. Her normal, friendly smile is missing, replaced by a scowl. It's the same look my best friend Todd's mom used to give me when I would come in from skateboarding wearing a dress.

"I always wore shorts underneath," I grumble as my shaky hands pick up the glass to take a drink.

Donna's expression suddenly changes to confused. "What?"

"Never mind." Placing the drink back down, I take a deep breath and try to center myself again. I want to believe this isn't happening, but it is. Or it did. I'm not sure which quite yet. Is it over? He said his sister is looking forward to meeting me. That means I need to get mentally prepared to meet Spencer Garrison again. Oh boy. I might need a Xanax for this. Or at least to get out of these heels. The chances of me faceplanting have skyrocketed.

Donna waits for me to finally make eye contact before asking the question I was hoping to avoid. "Wanna tell me what that was about?"

Like a deer in the headlights, I do what comes naturally. Avoid, avoid, avoid. "I don't know what you're talking about."

Pursing her lips, she clearly isn't buying it. No one ever said sales was my strong suit. "Adi . . ."

"Fine." I throw my hands up and take a deep breath. "I just freaked out, okay? Do you know who that was?"

"Hopefully my next cover model."

I lean forward and hiss, "That was Spencer Garrison. Five-time X Games gold medalist and skateboarding legend. He has sponsors all over the world and has started a foundation to bring extreme sports to underprivileged kids to help ward off health problems and give them an outlet for their energy. He's like, he's like . . ."

Her eyes get wide as I search for the words. "He's your muse!"

I press my lips tightly together, willing myself to play it off right. "No. No he is not."

"Yes he is!" she practically squeals. Clearly, I need to add acting lessons to my to-do list. "I've seen the online discussions. People have been trying for years to figure out where you get your inspiration from, but his name has never come up because you've never written about skateboarding. And this is why, right? You didn't want anyone to find out."

She is a little too excited about figuring out my deepest, darkest secret.

"Adi, this is amazing! Your muse's sister is a super fan! Do you know what this means?"

"My world is coming crashing down around me?"

She points at me with another smile on her face. "HA! You just admitted I'm right. No. This means you have an in with him. It means you can get the exclusive with him for all the covers you want. Plus, can you imagine the kind of marketing you can do?"

I feel my breathing get heavy again. "No. No way will I ever do marketing with Spencer Garrison. Just .

. . no."

Her face falls because Donna doesn't get it. She's beautiful and smart and confident. She could flirt her way out of a paper bag. I'm just me. Nerdy girl with a love of bright Converse shoes and '50s vintage style. I love architecture and history and watching the X Games with my equally nerdy best friend, Todd. I have a pen name for a reason—to keep me hidden because I don't want this kind of attention. "Adeline Snow" has a hard-enough time keeping the dorkiness at bay. "Agnes Sylvester" will screw it all up and make me look like a complete fool.

But of course Donna has one of the strongest business minds in the industry and doesn't let go of her ideas easily.

"Well, we'll just table this discussion for later." She picks up a menu and opens it, pretending to be looking through all the lunch options, when really, I'm sure the cogs in her brain are spinning at a rapid pace. "For now, let's just have a nice lunch and get you mentally prepared for the signing, okay?"

I nod and grab my own menu, knowing there is literally no way to prepare me for another meeting with Spencer Garrison. Even if his sister has only one book and I can be done with her in thirty seconds, there is a high probability I can make that thirty seconds the most uncomfortable of all our lives.

•••

Donna did most of the talking during our hour-long lunch and honestly, I'm not sure what it was about.

Something to do with her new release. I think it's a complete reverse on the stereotypical broody billionaire romance with a woman as the one with the cash. That sounds like something Donna would write, and she'll pull it off well.

But truthfully, most of my thoughts were about conversation starters for when the man, who I've inserted into every romantic idea of my life, and of course his sister show up at my table. At first, I was wishing the universe to strike them down with a twelve-hour flu bug, but then my Catholic guilt kicked in and I started praying for forgiveness.

I'm a mess.

I think I've come up with a few ideas. Basic things like: "Hi. How are you?" "How was your flight?" and "Would you like to give me babies?" I'm desperately hoping that last one is not the one that pops out of my mouth, but with me, you never know.

I've been going through the motions for the last however long, signing books for fans and that's helped. Seeing them just as nervous as I am has calmed me a bit. Like we're all in the same boat. The assistant who was assigned to me has only looked at me strange twice, so I assume I haven't spouted off too much weird stuff.

Looking up at the next reader, I find myself smiling back at an adorable woman wearing a shirt covered in books that reads "I'm in a serious relationship . . . with books". She looks so delighted to be here, like it's Christmas morning. I love being part of giving her that feeling.

"Hi, how are you?" I ask kindly and hold out my

hand. "I'm Adeline Snow."

She grabs my hand and shakes it vigorously. "Oh my gosh, it's so nice to meet you. I'm Kate, and I think I'm one of your biggest fans."

I laugh at her boisterous attitude. I like her already. I could use some of her energy. She'd be better than a Red Bull.

Handing me her first book, I take it and try to personalize it a little bit like I always do. "To Kate, So great to meet my biggest fan!" followed by my scribbled signature.

"I hope it's okay that I have more than one book," she says, looking a bit flustered and nervous as she pulls more paperbacks from her cart. "It's been my dream to meet you for so long I didn't want to waste the opportunity."

"No, it's fine," I respond, ignoring my assistant who is rolling her eyes. I know she was told there was a three-book limit, but if I'm the biggest celebrity in someone's life, I want them to walk away feeling special, not like I shuffled them through.

Her face lights up as she hands me another book. "Oh thank you. I just love your books. I've grown up around extreme sports so when I found your books, it was like every teenage fantasy come to life for me."

"Me too," I admit. "My best friend and I used to have X Games parties complete with face paint and streamers."

"Have you ever been to the games?" she asks, handing me yet another book.

I shake my head. "No. But I'm thinking I might need to next time they're in my neck of the woods."

"Oh my gosh you should! My brother gets me tickets every time, so if you need help navigating your way around or meeting some of the athletes, I'm your girl!"

She looks so excited, she misses the puzzle pieces clicking together in my brain. I just know the complete picture is about to come together in 3 . . . 2 . . . 1 . . .

"There you are."

And there he is.

Spencer Garrison.

My muse.

My dreamboat.

My fantasy come to life.

The only man I have ever hoped to never meet.

I chance a glance over at Donna, who of course is watching this entire exchange happen while also interacting with her own readers. She winks at me, simulates taking a deep breath no doubt as a reminder for me to not pass out, and turns back to her line, smiling wide in greeting.

Breathe, Aggi. Breathe.

"Oh! I was looking for you," Kate says to her brother. *Her brother.* Of course my muse's sister is my biggest fan. You can't make this stuff up. "I know you met Adeline Snow in the hallway earlier, but I was just telling her she should come out to the next X Games. You could show her around, maybe introduce her to people, right?"

He looks at me, with those deep blue eyes, and I can hardly concentrate on what I'm doing. "Uh, yeah. Sure."

"Great! Just track me down when you need to get hold of him." Kate continues to babble, completely unaware that my brain has basically stopped working. Then she slaps herself on the forehead. "Oh my gosh, who am I kidding? You won't know how to find me. I'll just email your assistant when we get close to the games and she can either hook us up or tell me to buzz off. That's probably better, right? Adeline?"

I snap out of my thoughts so quickly that I forget how to sign my own name and somehow end up scribbling "probably better" across Kate's book.

"Oh shoot. I'm sorry, I got distracted." Understatement of the year. If the hair standing on the back of my neck is any indication, Spencer is still staring at me. Probably because I'm acting like a total freak around him. "Let me grab you another copy."

"No!" Kate yells and then says sheepishly, "No, it's actually perfect. I love that it's not exact. It's like this moment in time has been immortalized. I know that sounds weird, but it's why I don't buy signed books online. For me, it's the moment I'll never forget."

She blushes prettily, and I'm hit hard by her words. This moment right here has been immortalized for her, like it's been immortalized for me because of her brother. This is her dream come true, and I'm ruining it by being stuck in my head. Even if she doesn't know it, I do.

Taking a deep breath, I look at her, really look at

her and smile. "I absolutely agree with you. And I appreciate your take on this moment so much." Closing the book and handing it to her, I add, "And yes, please email my assistant when it's closer to the games. I'd love to meet up for coffee or a meal."

Kate beams at me. "Really?"

"Of course! I always have time for my biggest fan."

She squeals and bounces on her toes. "Oh thank you! So much. Oh! Before I forget, can we get a picture?"

"Absolutely." I stand up and walk around my table, determined to keep my focus where it needs to be . . . on my reader and not her super-hot, I-want-him-to-father-my-babies brother. I'm sure she wouldn't appreciate my thoughts on him.

But as I should expect, my good intentions come to a screeching halt. As I walk around my table, my heel gets snagged on the bottom of my banner and down I go . . .

Right into Spencer Garrison's very strong, very muscular, very good smelling arms.

So much for my focus.

Chapter 6

Spencer

I stood back watching my sister in line for Adeline Snow like the awkward teenager I used to be. The woman sitting at the table with her readers is not the same woman I spoke with in the hallway a few hours ago. This woman, the smiling and engaging beauty who laughs along with her fans, is fascinating. I can't take my eyes off her. Well, and she's gorgeous. And slightly awkward still. There was a moment I was sure she was talking to herself, but she raised her chin, threw her shoulders back, and put on her game face.

I know it well. It's one I've mastered over the years. Being a professional athlete has its perks but also its downfalls. The biggest perk is doing things like this trip with my sister or buying my mom a house in the country. Traveling and meeting celebrities was the highlight of my teenage years and dating models and other athletes a huge upside to my early twenties. Now, as an almost thirty-year-old man, it's doing things for my family that I consider the perks.

The downsides haven't changed though. There

have always been the typical offerings: parties, women, drugs, and living life a little wilder than most. I never found myself too far into any of those situations. That has mostly been attributed to my extreme dislike of publicity, fame, and all the brown-nosing and kissing up that comes with that. Sure, I have a few sponsorships that require me to do some publicity and work with photographers, and Freddy is always up my ass for some red-carpet event, but social media, interviews, and public speaking are low on my list of priorities.

Watching Adeline, I have a strong suspicion she is the same way. If I know anything, it's how exhausting being "on" can be. If I were a betting man, I'd say she goes back to her hotel room after a long day of signing books and taking pictures with her fans, flips on the television, orders room service, and doesn't reappear for at least eighteen hours. At least, that's what I do.

When Kate is about three people from the front, I begin making my way toward the line. I know my role here today, and it isn't holding up this wall with my back, it's taking Kate's picture with the authors, and pulling that damn cart when necessary. A cart. Ridiculous.

By the time I reach the line, Kate is setting a stack of books back in the cart. Somehow, I know she has more.

"There you are."

"Oh! I was looking for you," Kate says to me. I recognize that excited gleam in her eye. She's in heaven, and I'm going to have a hell of a time getting her out those doors before this event is over. "I know you met

Adeline Snow in the hallway earlier, but I was just telling her she should come out to the next X Games. You could show her around, maybe introduce her to people, right?"

I look up at the woman in question and something about her expression makes me freeze up. It's like a mixture of awe and fear. "Uh, yeah. Sure."

"Great! Just track me down when you need to get hold of him." Kate continues to babble, so I tune her out, too focused on the woman in front of me. She's intriguing, to say the least. Awkward and unsure, yet comfortable around chatterboxes like my sister. Then all of the sudden, she appears to straighten her spine and laser focuses on the conversation in front of her. I shuffle over a few inches, putting myself in her line of sight again. Why I move, I have no idea, but it bothers me that she's ignoring me.

That's a really strange feeling to have about some random romance author I never knew existed until about three hours ago.

I tune back into the conversation just as Adeline is working her way around the table to stand in front of a large banner with her name on it. Thankfully she isn't like a few of the other authors I've seen around here with half naked dudes on the banners. I don't need to be that up-close and personal with a guy's nipples.

Kate looks over her shoulder for me but it's the sight of Adeline falling that has me rushing to her and scooping her in my arms before she falls to the ground. She's light in my arms and the gasp she gives followed by the "Karma is a bitch" she grumbles makes me chuckle.

"Whoa there," I say as I tighten my grip on her. Looking down, I see her heel is tangled in the base of the banner. I adjust my hold on her with my left hand and glide my right down her calf to grip her ankle. With a tug, I set her foot free but not before I note the goosebumps all over her skin and the light pink blush on her cheeks.

"You okay?"

Nodding, she stands up and takes a deep breath. Her eyes are fixated on my chest while my hands grip her waist. On reflex, my fingers widen, and my grip strengthens just a bit. She smells amazing. Like lemon and sugar. Slowly her gaze rises from my chest to meet my eyes. Smiling, I watch as her eyelashes flutter and her blush darkens.

Damn, she's beautiful.

"Sss . . .sorry. I'm fine. Thank you for saving me. That could have been disastrous."

"Ohmygod Adeline, are you okay? Spencer, let her go. Quit manhandling her," Kate admonishes as she pushes me out of the way. I stand awkwardly to the side, never taking my eyes off Adeline as my sister runs her hands down her arms and moves her around like one of her kids after they eat shit on the sidewalk.

"I'm fine, thank you so much for checking on me, Kate. How about that picture?"

"What? Oh, yes. Okay. Umm, Spence can you take it?"

Nodding, I pull Kate's phone from my back pocket

and snap a few pictures of the two of them. After the last photo, Kate steps back from Adeline. On impulse, I snap one more photo of Adeline talking to Kate and without thinking, text it to my phone.

"Wait!" Kate exclaims as Adeline turns to walk back around to her seat. "Will you take one more, with my brother?"

I watch as Adeline stumbles a little. Clearly flustered, I can't help but laugh a little at her awkwardness. It's fucking adorable.

"Sure," she says with a forced smile.

I switch places with Kate and stand next to Adeline awkwardly, nerves suddenly getting the best of me. Rubbing my now sweaty palms on my shorts, I move to place my arm around Adeline's waist when she stiffens.

Leaning down to her ear, I whisper, "I promise not to bite. Just smile so my sister will move along. Otherwise, she may invite you over for pot roast, and she's a horrible cook." That last comment earns me a giggle and ultimately a smile as she looks up at me through her long lashes.

"Perfect! Thank you so much, Adeline. I'll email your assistant about the games."

With a few more goodbyes and me calling Kate a "line hog," I manage to maneuver my sister away from her favorite author and into the abyss of this event. Lord help me.

•••

Two hours.

That's how long I lasted in the large room filled with dedicated and loyal fans. I had a few other words to describe the women I met today but that is the description Kate demanded I use when talking about her fellow readers. While I wasn't the lone man holding the handle to a rolling cart filled with books, I'm sure I was the only one who was less than two months post-op from his second knee surgery. By the time my knee swelled to the size of a small melon, I had already made eye contact with a few guys who had also entered the Twilight Zone also known as a book signing.

When we were in line for an author that my sister declared to be *the* author for ugly cry books, I looked to the man on my right, and he rolled his eyes in time with me. Solidarity. We were men, there in solidarity, supporting the women we love, one photo and two lip balms at a time.

Unfortunately for Kate, my body wasn't on board with my role as support system, and I had to abandon my duties and hobble to the bar. A few beers, a basket of wings, and a college football game later, she appeared to retrieve me for phase two of the day—dinner. I had a bad feeling the "dedicated and loyal" readers she met in line throughout the day were going to be at this dinner and was thinking of a million excuses to avoid going. Looking down at my knee as she pushed the button for the elevator, I realized the bum knee was not a viable excuse.

"Stop trying to get out of this. I'm taking *you* to dinner to thank you. Seriously, Spence, this was the best birthday gift ever. I had such an amazing day. I mean, we talked to Adeline Snow for like ten minutes."

Laughing, I pull the rolling cart into the elevator behind me before answering. "It was more like fifteen, and by the way the others in line reacted, it may have been longer. And, you're welcome."

"I've been in her reader group for a while now and admit to freely stalking her social media, but she doesn't post many photos of herself. That girl does like her coffee though. Anyway, I had no idea how pretty she was until you stopped her in the hallway."

I listen to my sister ramble on as the elevator ascends to our floor. Thoughts of Adeline Snow and her beauty fill my head. It was her quirky outfit and obvious awkwardness that I liked the most. And her smile. That damn smile.

"Is that okay?"

"What?" I ask, completely missing anything Kate had been saying.

"I said I want to take a quick shower before we go."

"Oh yeah, that's fine. What are you going to do with all of these books?"

Kate slides the key card in front of the sensor a few times before the light turns green, granting us access. As we step in the room, she asks, "What do you mean?"

"Are you going to read them all?"

"Oh, I've already read most of them."

Say what? Why would we stand in line all day for her to purchase books she's read?

"I'm so confused," I say as I drop the handle of the cart and throw myself on my bed, careful not get my shoes on the bedspread. Although come to think of it, this probably isn't the safest place to be lying down. I'm sure there are way worse germs on this top blanket than the ones on my shoes.

Rolling her eyes as she stands at the foot of the bed, hands on her hips, she lets out a loud exhale.

"I read most of my books on my e-reader, but I get my favorites signed and have them all on my bookshelves. I'm a book nerd, Spencer, this shouldn't be news to you."

She's right, for our entire life Kate has been an avid reader. I just never realized to what level. I kick off my shoes as I settle into the pillows, back resting against the headboard as Kate gathers her belongings and heads into the bathroom for her shower.

"I'll be quick, promise." Famous last words as she closes the door. I know I have at least an hour. Looking around for the remote, I spy her e-reader instead. It would be wrong of me to read one of her books. That has to be some sort of invasion of privacy. What if, instead, I sneak one of those books in the cart? She'd never know. That's probably better.

I furrow my brow at my own weird thoughts because how in the world would reading a book be an invasion of privacy? I must need to ice my knee more. Clearly the pain is making my brain malfunction.

Like Kate has some sort of sixth sense, probably a mom thing, the door opens, and she peeks her head out to say, "Do not touch my paperbacks. They are not for reading. There's no passcode on my device. Just stay out of the folder that says "bow chicka wow wow" if you know what's good for you."

I shake away the idea of what is in that folder as I grab her device and lie back down on the bed. Sliding my finger across the screen, I watch as it lights up and no less than a dozen folders appear on the screen. As I skim the folders I see she has many of them named the various genres she mentioned earlier when she was explaining the different types of romance. One folder in particular catches my eye. *Adeline Snow.*

Curiosity may kill the cat, but in my case, I hope it only helps me understand how a quirky woman with a throwback hairdo and a skirt that looks like it's missing a poodle can write anything that involves Extreme Sports. As the folder opens, little books appear and fill the screen. Clicking one that depicts a snowboarder, I try to leave my judgments at the door as I see what Ms. Snow has to offer.

"What'd you choose?" Kate asks, scaring the shit out of me.

"Jesus, what are you? A ninja? And how did you get ready so fast?"

"First of all, it's been an hour like I told you it would be."

Glancing at the clock I realize she's right. Huh. Adeline Snow has some real talent for me to lose track of time.

"And second, I'm a mom. I can move in and out of a room on demand without being detected. If I couldn't, I'd never get any peace. Or wine. So which book did you choose?" Kate asks, grabbing the device from my hand and tapping the screen. "Oh, one of Adeline's books. I loved this one. I wanted to have fictional babies with Gabe. He's swoony."

"Fictional babies? Swoony? What the hell are you talking about?"

Dismissing me with a hand wave, she turns to slide her feet into her shoes before grabbing her purse.

"Nevermind. So, what do you think?"

"I think there's not one reference to a bosom or throbbing member on any of these pages."

"It's not our momma's romance, dipshit. Or hell, even Gran's. This is real-life romance. Broken people who deserve second chances and true love."

"If you say so. I will give Ms. Snow credit, she's on point with the sports."

"I know, right? It's like she was either an athlete in a previous life or she does her homework. Actually, she did say she grew up watching the X Games. I guess authors do write what they know," she rambles. "But, if you really want to enjoy her books, you need to get the audios."

"The whats?"

"Audio books. The guy who narrates them is amazing. His voice . . . well, let's just say he may be why you have a third niece."

I flash her an over-exaggerated grimace. "And on that note, let's go to dinner. I think I'll get the steak and lobster after that comment. It may help bleach my brain."

Chapter 7

Aggi

Scrubbing the makeup off my face, I try to forget about the day. Normally, I'm exhausted after a signing, but today was over the top for my emotions. I felt like I was riding a roller coaster . . .

Anticipation of meeting all my readers.

Unexpected adrenaline and fear as my muse approached me.

Recovery time to pull myself back together.

Small drop of adrenaline as I made conversation with readers.

Huge adrenaline and fear as my muse approached again.

Literal drop into his arms, leaving me with a third huge shot of adrenaline.

Attempting to get my breathing under control until I could get off that wild ride.

If I could figure out how to make it work, the entire thing could be a cool storyline. Too bad I don't write about my own life and experiences. Not that I have enough experiences to draw from anyway. I really need someone close to me to start dating so they can give me some inspiration.

Looking into the mirror, droplets of water slide down my face. What is it that makes me so awkward around people? I'm a decent looking person, right? Maybe more on the handsome than pretty side, but all the acne from my younger years went away long ago with a strict routine of several glasses of water every day and some basic facewash. My big, dark eyes are framed by thick lashes and not a smile line, or crow's feet as they're so affectionately called, yet. Even I have to admit, I have nice thick hair. The dark isn't showing any signs of gray popping through and usually it does what I want. Unless it's windy. Or humid. Or raining.

Okay, sometimes it's a struggle, but hairbands were invented for a reason.

So why can I not seem to conjure up a conversation with strangers without almost having a panic attack first?

I suppose it really isn't my looks that make me awkward. It's the words that come out of my mouth. There's a random disconnect between my brain and my tongue. Not to mention my clumsiness. I should be grateful I only fell once today.

Wait . . . twice.

Well, three times if you count when my hotel room door flew open faster than I was expecting, but since no one was here to see it, I'm choosing to forget that one.

Patting my face with a dry towel and finishing up my facial-care regimen, I try to focus on the important things about today: my favorite Olaf footie pajamas that feel soft against my skin and the room service that will be here in fifteen minutes. After expending so much emotional energy today, downtime sounds perfect. As an introvert, I need to recuperate.

Plopping down on my bed, I grab my laptop and open my latest manuscript. Maybe "manuscript" is giving it too much credit. "Random word doc with a few paragraphs slapped on" is a more fitting description.

Set in California, our hero is a newly retired surfing instructor with a new protégé in the form of our beautiful, yet broken heroine. Trying to make a comeback after a severe injury, it's up to our hero to help her get her head on straight and get back into competition form. Can he help save her career, or will their emotions get in the way and destroy it all?

Happy with the premise, I place my fingers on the keyboard and wait.

And wait.

And wait some more.

Gah! Why won't the words come? What is going on with my brain that is causing my creativity to stall out so badly? If nothing else, I figured seeing Spencer in the flesh would give me a boost of inspiration. Now that I've seen him up close, smelled him, felt his heat when he wrapped his arm around my waist for a picture, I should be cranking this story out quickly.

Closing my eyes, I think back to how he looked at me. Deep blue eyes that seemed to see right into my soul. His scent reminded me of my younger years when the possibilities were endless, and I was free of adult responsibilities, my only goal to have fun and master the halfpipe. His strong arms that made me feel petite and safe.

It seems so easy in my head but getting those thoughts onto this page isn't happening.

Sighing, I toss my laptop to the side and grab my phone to dial. Contrary to popular belief, working as an author isn't just writing. There's a lot of administrative work that goes into it as well. Maybe I can be productive in that arena until I'm finally hit with words that turn into a story.

"Hey there, *Adeline*," a sexy voice says on the other end of the phone.

"Shut up, Todd. You know I hate it when you call me that."

The deep timber of his voice reverberates through the phone as he laughs. "Sorry. I didn't realize you already scrubbed Adeline off your face and morphed back into Aggi. Are you already in your jammies?"

I snuggle down under the covers of my king-sized bed and sigh again. "Yeah. It was a long day."

"I saw."

"Saw? What do you mean you saw?" Now I'm confused. He's at home and I'm in Chicago, right?

"Do you ever check your social media accounts?"

Sitting straight up in bed, I grab my laptop again and frantically begin to log on. I have a bad feeling about this. "Not unless I have to. Why? What happened?"

"You are so about to freak out. I'll wait." He chuckles again and the sound of it reminds me of the reason for my call—to find out if he got the contract worked out with my publisher to start narrating my latest novel. Since we were kids, I told Todd he needed to get into radio, but he wasn't interested. And thank goodness for that. Suddenly, with internet and satellite, local radio seems to be a dying art. Audiobooks, though, are on the rise.

With Todd's background as a high school and college theater geek, I finally convinced him to take a shot at narration. Lots of actors do it to bring in some cash on the side while they wait for their big break. So he went for it and like I had predicted, his audition blew my publishers away. Honestly, it blew me away too. If he wasn't my best friend and, well, *Todd*, I would have told him he was a sex pot.

But he is my best friend so ew. No.

None of that matters right now, though, as I open my social media page and see hundreds of notifications. That's not unusual, but normally I'm tagged on pictures of my covers or a graphic someone made. That's not what I'm seeing this time.

Nope. This time it's all pictures of me and Spencer.

Me staring at him awkwardly in the hallway.

Me staring at Spencer like a deer in headlights

while sitting behind my table at the signing.

Me falling into his arms.

I keep scrolling until I see it . . . the actual video of me falling into his arms. Because of course someone filmed it.

Groaning, I toss my laptop aside again and throw myself on the bed, pulling the blanket over my face to hide.

"Seriously, Aggi, that video was priceless," Todd jokes, making me want to choke him until his little red head pops off. "I don't know why you always wear heels to those things."

"My publicist makes me!" I argue.

"Then she either doesn't know you very well or she doesn't like you very much. I'm surprised you haven't gotten a concussion."

"Shut up, Todd. I like my Betty Page look. It's like my own personal Comic-Con every time I sign."

His laughter is starting to irritate me. He's my best friend and I'll forgive him, but even he doesn't know what Spencer means to me. I mean, is to me. I mean . . . I don't know what I mean because Spencer Garrison shouldn't be anything to me. He should be right back in the little box in my brain marked "fantasy" that is only opened when I'm on a deadline. But no. Now I can't get that box closed because the fantasy has come to life.

Well, the man has anyway. The fantasies are never actually going to come to fruition.

Todd's voice breaks through my thoughts and I try to focus back on the conversation. "No seriously, though. Did he skate up to your table? Was he wearing a medal?"

I roll my eyes. "No and no."

"Did you ask him about his rehab at least? Is he going to be able to compete any time soon?"

"I don't know."

"What do you mean you don't know, Aggi?"

"I mean, I don't know, *Todd*," I retort, using my best Julia Louis-Dreyfus voice from National Lampoon's Christmas Vacation.

"Well you should have asked, *Margot*."

We both burst out laughing at our ridiculousness. This is why I'm awkward in social situations. I've got Todd egging on my weirdo side daily. Good thing he's the best friend a girl could ask for, because he may be the only one left at some point if I can't get myself under control.

When we calm down, he starts with the inquisition again. I hate it, but I also know my meeting Spencer Garrison is huge news for a skateboarding fan like Todd.

"Seriously, Aggi. Did you talk to him at all or did you freeze up?"

Throwing the blanket off my head, I take a deep breath of cool air. "I didn't ask him anything about skateboarding. I didn't ask him anything at all."

"What? Why not?"

"I don't know. First, I froze. But then I realized it wasn't really the right time. His sister is a huge reader, and she was kind of having her own fan girl moment . . ."

"His sister?" he interrupts. "Is she single?"

Shaking my head, I murmur. "Ohmygod, you're such a pig."

"Hey, I have eyes. Spencer Garrison is an attractive guy. I bet his sister is as hot as he is."

"She is, but I think I overheard her saying something about taking a load of books out to her minivan, so I assume she's filling up her vehicle with kids too."

"Dammit," he says under his breath. "The good ones are always taken."

"Anyway," I say forcefully, trying to get him back on track, "I wanted to know if you started voicing my book yet."

"No." His voice suddenly quiets as he stops being so ornery and gets down to business. "I spent the day setting up my new home studio."

I sit up in bed, only this time it's because I'm excited for my friend. "Really? How does it look?"

"Like a padded closet?"

I snort a laugh. "So it can double as your emotional support room if you need one."

"Dammit. I knew I should have bought some of the supplies with my FSA. Think my insurance company will reimburse me?"

"I doubt it. Nice try, though."

"I can't wait for you to see it. When are you coming home, anyway?"

Twisting a stray strand of hair around my finger, I run through my mental calendar. "It's going to be a few more days. I have one more small signing in LA."

"What are you talking about? I barely have my studio set up, let alone started my narration of this book. Are you promoting it already?"

His confusion makes me laugh. "Oh, sweetie, what you're working on is my release a few months from now. I'm finishing up the promo for the book that released last month."

"Don't "sweetie" me, Agnes." Jerk. He knows I hate that name. "I thought you were done since you're on a deadline."

"You know I hate when you use my full name. And I am on deadline."

He laughs but it's less humorous and more confused. "How many books are you working on?"

"No idea. Four traditionally." I tick them off on my fingers. "One that just released, one that's going to release in a couple months, one in the final editing stages, and one I'm writing. But I promised my editor another indie by the end of the year."

"Girl, you're a mess. But I love ya. So this signing you're going to . . ."

I groan at the reminder. Right now the last thing I want to do is think about being in front of that many people again.

"Oh you're going to have so much fun. Maybe Spencer will make a random appearance."

Grimacing when my finger gets tangled in my hair, I struggle to get it free while ignoring Todd's comment about Spencer. "Hopefully it won't be too bad. I think it's only me at a bookstore, so minus the walking part and I guess the talking part, I should be okay. I can just do a Q&A or something. That's not as bad as doing a panel where I have to sound intelligent."

"You're always intelligent, Aggi." I smile at his kind words. "You just *sound* like an idiot while public speaking."

My smile drops as someone knocks on my door.

"Well, on that friendly insulting note, I need to go. Room service is here."

Scrambling off the bed, my mouth waters at the thought of the cheeseburger and fries waiting for me on the other side of the door. All that adrenaline has made me hungry.

"I knew you had your footie pajamas on already!" Todd shouts through the speaker.

"Bye, Todd!" I yell back and hang up as the sound of him laughing again comes through. Tossing the phone on my bed I call out, "I'm coming!" and dance my way over to the door. Seriously. Almost nothing makes me happier than a big greasy burger. Except eating a big greasy burger in bed.

Throwing the door open, I push my black rimmed glasses up higher on my nose and smile at the porter.

"Ms. Sylvester?" he asks politely.

"That's my name, don't wear it out."

That earns me a furrowed brow and a "Well. Okay."

Awkwaaaaard.

Clearing my throat, I try to reel my excitement back in. "Yeah. So anyway, I'll just take this tray off your cart. They added the tip onto my account already, right?"

"Yes, ma'am," he says as I take the tray, and he rolls the cart out of the way. "Can I get you anything else?"

As I open my mouth to answer, I glance at the person walking by. I know those arms. My eyes widen as I realize who it is.

Spencer Garrison glances over, away, and then does a double take when he realizes who I am. So of course I do the only reasonable thing I can . . .

I slam the door in the poor porter's face, never answering his question.

Crap.

I better call downstairs and ask them to add another ten bucks to his tip.

Chapter 8

Spencer

My flight this morning was much more enjoyable than the one I took a few days ago. Not only was I not folded up like a taco but there weren't two people in a battle of wills on either side of me. Instead, I have an empty seat next to me and enough leg room I can stretch my knee. Who knew spending a few days with my sister fangirling all over a bunch of romance authors would be so exhausting?

And interesting.

Not only did I see a different side to Kate, but I met some pretty cool ladies too. And one in particular who keeps running through my mind.

Adeline Snow.

After Kate basically word vomited all over her about the games and promises of getting her tickets or behind the scenes I didn't think I'd see her again. Sure, I may have downloaded an app so I could check out one of her books. I fly a lot, I need something to distract me. But, that's as far as I thought it would go.

Then, walking down the hall after dinner, I saw a porter standing outside a door with a cart and glanced toward the door.

Standing with a silver domed plate in her hand was a woman dressed in footy pajamas and wearing a pair of glasses. It wasn't the footies or the glasses that caught my attention; it was the look of horror on the woman's face as the door slammed. It was that move that made me laugh to myself and download the rest of her books after I returned to the room. It isn't like I can take Kate's e-reader with me to finish the book I started. If she was going to freak out about seeing me, I had to know a little more about her writing.

Now, I sit with a bottle of water in the cup holder to my right, my knee stretched out and a book about a BMX rider on my phone. I'm reading a fucking romance novel about a dude who could easily be me if you swapped out the bike for a skateboard. Only, never in my life have I encountered a woman who saw past the fame, the trophies, and the money like the woman in this book. Nope. The Pro Ho's as they're typically called are usually all about the fame, the notoriety, and the money. Not that I'm a billionaire or anything. But with my sponsorships I definitely do all right.

By the time the captain alerts us to the descent into Los Angeles, I'm so engrossed in this story I missed the flight attendant scooping up my empty bottle or the last opportunity to hit the bathroom before we land. Great.

Thankfully, it's a smooth landing, and I know this airport like the back of my hand. Freddy's offices are here in LA, and I feel like he's always dragging me here for either a contract negotiation or fundraising event. I don't mind the fundraising, even if I'm dressed like a penguin, it's the contracts and inevitable photo shoots that follow that I hate. In particular, the underwear campaign he convinced me was "life changing." Oh, it was life changing all right. Changed me right into a cardboard cutout in department stores across the country. Hence, the Pro Ho's I deal with.

Joke was on him though. When I agreed to that campaign, I insisted he work out a publishing deal for one of the women who works with my foundation. She'd shared her desire to publish a series of children's books and asked if I would lead the campaign and approve the use of a character inspired by me for the books. I agreed—without Freddy's approval—and that cardboard cutout I'm proud of.

As the seat belt light signals we're free to move around the cabin, I exit the reading app on my phone and rise to grab my bag from the overhead bin. Exiting the plane, I smile at the flight attendants and pause when one lifts her hand and says, "I didn't want to make it awkward during the flight, but I'm a huge fan." Sure she is.

"Thank you." My response is polite but short.

"Maybe, while you're in LA, we can . . . ." she begins, but before she can continue, I smile and keep walking. Nope. Hard pass on whatever she's selling. I'm going to be in LA for three days and then I'm heading home to Lexington. I didn't build that house for shits and giggles.

Quickly making my way down the jetway, I find the nearest restroom and handle business before rushing to the curbside pickup and the car I know is waiting for me. The airport in Los Angeles is huge and it's easy to get lost in the sea of people. Thank goodness. Of course, being tall makes me stand out regardless, but here I'm just some guy walking toward a dark sedan.

"Good afternoon, sir," the driver says as he slowly pulls away from the curb.

"Hello. Do you have the address for the facility?"

"Yes, I do. My instructions state you are to be dropped off for your appointment at two o'clock and then I'll return to pick you up at three fifteen, at which time I will then drive you to Mr. Logan's office."

"Any chance you can swing through a drive through for some food? I'm starving, and if I know anything about the appointment I'm headed to, I'll need the fuel."

●●●

I may bitch about coming to LA, and for the most part, I'm serious. But, the silver lining to the days here is the PT guy Freddy hooked me up with. Jimmy is badass, and while I want to nut punch him for pushing me, I know I'll be better for the hard work. Plus, he's funny as hell and we get along like we've been friends for years. But, he also leaves me alone while I'm working and observes more than interferes. It's why I'm able to finish the book I was reading on the plane.

Yeah, I downloaded the audiobook too. It was less than two dollars because I bought the e-book. These authors and the people who make audio books are genius when it comes to marketing. A simple "Buy this book for four bucks and then get the audio for only two more. It's a steal!" had me purchasing without question.

What I hadn't planned when I started this book was the very detailed sex scenes. By detailed I mean hot. Thankfully, the big dude staring at me while I finish the last minute on the bike manages to dampen any horniness the woman narrating was stirring up inside me.

Jimmy continues to stare at me, eyes wide as I pedal. What the hell? Pulling my earbuds from my ear, I look at him confused.

"Uh, bro what are you listening to?"

"A book. Why?" I ask.

"I figured it was either a book or you were on a call with a hottie on a one nine hundred number."

Confused, I tilt my head for him to continue. Jimmy takes a deep breath, eyes focused on the ceiling as he places his hands on his hips before opening his mouth and speaking at octave about three times higher than he should ever do again.

"I love when he rubs his cock against my wet—"

"Enough," I shout.

"I'm so full of desire I'm dripping—"

"Dude, shut up." I shout louder as I stand from my position. Stopping him from continuing. "How did— shit, my earbuds. How much did you hear?"

Instead of responding, Jimmy doubles over in the

most obnoxious bout of laughter I've ever witnessed. My irritation, and slight embarrassment, grows with each leg slap and gasp for breath. Sick of his theatrics, I grab my sweaty towel from around my shoulders and toss it at him, successfully smacking him in the face. "Gross. Look, I'm not judging, brother, but you look more in pain than turned on by that porn you're listening to. I have to admit I was getting into the story before I saw your face all scrunched up and red. It occurred to me that maybe it wasn't the story causing the pain but your knee."

I look like I'm in pain? "It's just tender is all. No worries man, but I need to stop anyway. Apparently, Freddy needs me, my fucking phone is blowing up, and it's messing with the book."

Nodding, Jimmy waves me over to the mat where he'll stretch me. I lower myself from the bike and as I walk toward him, I look down at my phone and see the number of notifications from one of my apps. It says ninety-nine plus. What the hell? I never have that many notifications. The text messages show five and the missed calls six.

Opting to pull up the texts first, I sit down on a mat and scroll to see who has been trying to get hold of me. Freddy's name has a two next to it, my mom's name has a one and Kate's a two. Tapping on my mom's first I read it twice, still not fully understanding what she's talking about.

Mom: You look so handsome. Bring her to dinner!

Bring who to what?

I tap Freddy's name next.

Freddy: I need a name for a background. You're supposed to clear this shit with me.

Freddy: Who is this chick? Why are people freaking out? Call me.

What the actual fuck is going on? Has everyone lost their mind?

Kate is next on my list and hopefully she has an explanation.

Kate: OMG! Can you believe the freaking picture is on the INTERNET! I had no idea anyone would see it.

Kate: Do you hate me? Please don't hate me. I assumed it was just your business profile. Do you even check that thing or use it? The last picture is of Santa. You need someone to work your social media. I love you. Don't hate me.

The little plus sign next to the ninety-nine on the social media app taunts me. I lower my finger and tap the icon and a list of notifications pops up. Comments, likes, tags, and reposts. What the hell is a repost? Tapping one of the notifications, I go to some random page and that's when I see it.

Me with Adeline Snow in my arms, her face peering up at me through those long dark lashes. It's the moment I caught her at the signing. On the internet. For everyone to see. Going back to the notifications I scroll until I see what I assume is the original post.

Kate.

No wonder she's worried I'm pissed. Pulling up her profile I see the caption she put with the picture and shake my head before I laugh. Only my sister. "Caught in the wild @Spence_G5 playing swoony hero to my #favoriteauthor @AdelineSnowWrites as he catches her. He's single ladies!" Then she has a bunch of dumb hashtags that make no sense to me. Damn there are a lot. What does #swoonyheroesarereal #ladiesbeware #sometimeshesanidiot mean?

"Dammit, Kate."

"Is that the woman's name?" Jimmy asks, drawing my attention from the phone.

"What?"

"In the picture. Your woman. Is her name Kate?"

"First, how have I been here an hour and you haven't said anything about this shit? Two, she's not my woman. And three, Kate is my sister. Or was. I may kill her. I've always wanted to be an only child."

Laughing, Jimmy motions for me to lie down. I do as instructed and try to regulate my heartbeat as a million thoughts about the shitstorm this is going to cause runs through my head. As he stretches my leg, my phone rings. *Freddy.*

"Hello?" I answer tentatively.

"This is fucking gold, Garrison. I'm already talking to her people, and we're going to ride this out for some major promotion. Now, finish up and get to my office. We have a lot of work to do."

Without letting me get a word in, the line goes dead and I toss my phone to the side with a groan. No promotion. I don't do promotion.

Chapter 9

Aggi

For a homebody, I enjoy traveling a lot. I know. I'm a walking conundrum.

But I love exploring new places and getting to experience new cultures. Venice Beach is certainly turning out to be a culture all its own.

I've been walking up and down the boardwalk for a couple hours, fascinated by the sights and sounds. The architecture alone is beautiful. With colorful arches and murals painted on buildings, it's a visual experience like I've never had before. My favorite is the giant mural of a skateboarder. I have at least two dozen pictures of it at different angles with different filters. Thank goodness for the cat fight over this Nikon during the after-Thanksgiving sale last year. While two grandmas decided to throw down, I reached around them and grabbed the last one and the extra lenses that were on sale. I may have then run to the cashier as fast as I could before they realized the item they were fighting over was gone.

It was the most exciting conflict I've ever been involved in, but so worth it for the pictures it's taken of this mural.

Wandering around the beach, I'm hoping to catch some surfing inspiration. Except for one or two people on boards who aren't very good, it's mostly just beach-goers. It's disappointing to say the least. Writer's block continues to kill my ability to get this manuscript done and the longer this goes on, the more off-track I'm getting.

I've already had one hard conversation with my publisher begging to push my deadline back. I highly doubt I'll get another extension. Sure, this release is well over a year away, but publishing houses love having everything in the can early, so they can market it for months. I understand the whys of it, but knowing does little to take the pressure off.

The water is beautiful, and I could stand here and take pictures all day, but this isn't helping me through the block. So, I pull up my GPS to chart a course to the place I know I'll be inspired—Venice Skate Park. If anywhere can help me sort the words out in my brain, that's probably it.

Heading back up to the boardwalk, I enjoy the sun on my face and the smell of the ocean. Living in the middle of Nowhere, USA, I don't hear waves often, so doing it here, with mountains in the distance, is a real treat.

The boardwalk is like nothing I've seen before. Re-tailers are selling everything from toe rings to medical marijuana to ice cream. All in brightly colored build-ings of all shapes and sizes. Dodging a tourist here and there I do my best to walk and take pictures at the same time. Considering my track record for being able to walk and chew bubble gum is already low, I'm impressed with myself. I haven't fallen or run into anyone. Yet.

Must be because I'm wearing my pink Converse instead of heels.

The bright colors really could distract me from my destination, but I do my best to not get sidetracked. There's so much to see. Although, I admit to taking a small detour when I see some palm trees that are spray painted. The graffiti art is striking against the blue background of the water and is definitely worth taking a few snapshots.

Finally, I hear the telltale sounds of boards hitting the pavement and my steps speed up. As I come to the railing and look out over the edge, I gasp.

It's the most beautiful concrete park I've ever seen. There are several large areas shaped like swimming pools but larger and deeper. In between and surrounding the bowls are areas with stairs, railings, and arches, all perfect for an avid skater to use to create magic with their board.

I find myself gawking as I take it all in. This is a skater's dream. Not only is the location amazing, but the park is designed for skaters of all levels, from novices to professionals. I'm practically itching to get out there myself. Too bad I threw away my last board when I was in my teens.

Actually, no. That was definitely the right thing to do. Being taken away in an ambulance when I inevitably got a concussion would ruin the cool vibe happening around here.

Bringing my camera to my face, I begin snapping shots rapidly. There are only a few skaters out right now, probably because it's the middle of a work day, but I'm not complaining. I watch through my lens when one particular athlete catches my eye. Tall and lean, he seems to be a favorite with all the other skaters. Whenever he stops at the top of the bowl, they all give him fist bumps and make conversation.

From here, he appears a bit older than everyone else. And yet, he seems the most comfortable with his skills.

I snap some shots as he bends down to give pointers to the lone child on the ramp. I can't hear them, but I imagine he's saying something like, "Make sure to bend deep on the aciddrop." Sure enough, the boy with a bright yellow helmet takes a deep breath and drops in the bowl, making it halfway up the other side before coming to a stop at the bottom.

Obviously, he's brand new to this, but by the cheers coming from the man who has my attention and the other guys, you'd think the kid just won a medal. I make sure to zoom in on the boy when he raises his arms and bellows in victory. Suddenly, I'm starting to feel more inspired for my story. Maybe Greer was right—maybe it's time for a single mom story. My surfer could work with kids, right? Maybe he's retired, and part of his new business includes programs for children.

I let the idea roll around in my brain while I watch the little dude move out of the way for the next person.

The older guy gets in position. Keeping my camera focused, I'm not stingy as I press the button and rapid fire the second he heads downhill.

This guy is amazing. The way he jumps, and spins and flies through the air. It's obvious he's been doing this for decades and just by how comfortable he is in the bowl, I wonder if he aspires to go pro. He certainly could hang with the big names. In fact, the way he moves reminds me a lot of Spencer Garrison.

I roll my eyes at myself. *Give me a break, Aggi. One chance meeting with Spencer Garrison doesn't mean you'll ever see him again,* then pushing my thoughts aside, I wait for him to launch above the rim in front of me. I'm at the perfect place to capture him mid-flight. With the ocean in the background, this is going to be a great picture. If I ever break my own rule and write a skater book, I could use it for a graphic.

Just as he comes over the top, I begin rapid firing again. He spins and turns, and his face comes into view.

Holy. Shit.

My camera falls from my face at the same time my jaw drops practically to the ground. How in the hell is Spencer Garrison the same place I am? Again?

Are the stars aligned against me? Was I a terrible person in a past life? It's because I took the last cheese and fruit box at my favorite coffee shop the other day instead of leaving it for someone else, isn't it?

Regardless, I should turn around and leave quickly before he sees me, but of course I'm practically glued to the ground. Because that's what Spencer Garrison does. He renders me speechless and movement-less. My only saving grace is that he hasn't seen me. I suppose I can stalk him for a little while longer. Because when will I ever get a chance to see him skate up-close and personal again? Never. That's when. Besides, the coifed hair and bright red lips are left behind in my hotel room. Regular Aggi doesn't look nearly as put together as Adeline Snow, so he'll never know I'm here.

Eyes glued to my muse as he makes his way around the bowl it suddenly makes sense why the other skaters have gravitated to the oldest guy out there. From an I-am-a-nervous-freak-of-nature standpoint, this is a horrible moment in time. But from a skating-obsessed standpoint, I can appreciate how exciting this must be for the guys on the other side of the rail. How many people can say they've skated with the great Spencer Garrison?

Probably hundreds, actually. But still. A sighting in the wild is always rare.

Something like this could be a fun scene for my book. Hmm.

I watch as Spencer comes back around the curve, pops up over the ledge and jumps off the board. He turns to me and smiles.

I look left, then right, then over my shoulder, there's no one around. Wait. Is he smiling at . . . *me*?

Spencer shakes his head and chuckles as he grabs his board and walks my direction.

Oh no. No, no, no, no. This isn't happening. My breathing picks up and if it doesn't slow down soon, my heart is liable to beat right out of my chest and gallop away.

Looking everywhere, except at Spencer, I avoid any eye contact. If I don't look at him, maybe he won't see me, right? RIGHT?!?

"You're Adeline Snow, aren't you?"

Looking away didn't work like I hoped. I close my eyes and take a deep breath, willing myself to say something intelligent like "That's me."

Instead, as I open my lids to look back at him, I freeze, mouth wide open. Of course.

I watch as Spencer comes closer, still smiling at me like I'm amusing. Because no one can pull off the marble statue look like I can.

Dropping his board to the ground, he places his hands on his hips, and narrows his eyes a bit against the sun, making the corners crinkle slightly. The movement does nothing to make him look less appealing. If anything, it makes him sexier.

"I'm going to make an observation," he begins. "For whatever reason, I make you really nervous, don't I?"

Somehow, my head moves up and down in response. This is good. It means I might not actually pass out. If only I could take a breath.

"My sister says you're a fan of the X Games, so I'm guessing you've watched me skate before."

I nod again only this time I force my jaw to shut. More progress.

"Is that why you're nervous around me?"

I shake my head and then realize if I had just nodded, he would have written me off as a super fan, not the crazy girl who can't seem to pull herself together when he's around. *Quick, Aggi, say something! Throw him off the trail!*

"I like skateboarding."

I mentally slap myself for sounding like an idiot again. This is not going well. Spencer chuckles while I take a deep breath, trying to pull myself together.

He's just a man, Aggi. A sexy, kind, beautiful man you want to jump . . . stop that! You don't know him well enough to jump him. Maybe just lick him . . . NO! Okay. Breathe. Act normal. Pretend he's a regular guy. Pretend he's Todd. Todd has a sexy voice and you talk to him. Just think of Todd . . . Todd . . . Todd . . .

"Todd is my best friend." Closing my eyes slowly, I shake my head at myself. Let's try this again. "That's not what I meant to say. What I meant to say was, how did you know it was me?" This time I pat myself on the back for sounding somewhat normal and asking a valid question.

Spencer takes it as invitation to move closer and stand next to me. We watch the other skateboarders as they practice some moves, cheering each other on. "How could I not know it was you?" he admits. "We met a couple times at the signing and then you slammed a door in my face."

Despite the playfulness of his tone, I groan at the memory. "I was hoping you would forget that part."

"I'll never forget that. The door actually bonked the porter on the tip of the nose." I gasp. "Oh, don't worry. It didn't hurt him at all. It literally just touched the tip of his nose. It was just so funny because it was perfect. Reminded me of that scene in Home Alone when Kevin is about to get run over by the van and it stops at the exact right moment."

"I love that movie." I also have no idea why I said that, but I suppose it's better than running away screaming, so we'll call it a win.

"It's a classic. I make sure to watch it at least once every December."

I can feel his eyes on me, but I refuse to look, instead keeping my eyes trained on the opposite side of the park. One of the taller guys, a man with long, dark limbs and even longer, darker dreads is picking up speed in the bowl. Around he goes several times before taking off up the side and . . . *Holy crap! He just jumped over the kid!*

"Did you see that?" I squeal in disbelief. Getting up over the lip without falling is hard enough. But to launch so high he ends up jumping over a person? "That was incredible!" Forgetting who I'm standing next to, I glance over at Spencer who has his eyes trained on me. My eyes widen, and my skin feels flush when I realized I grabbed his arm in my excitement. Quickly, I pull my hand away like I've been burned. He doesn't seem fazed. "Why are you looking at me like that?"

"I'm trying to get a better grasp on how to talk to you. If we're going on tour together, I figure we need to be comfortable communicating."

Somewhere in the background noise in my brain, a record player scratches to a stop. "We're doing what?"

"Going on tour?" I look at him blankly, half shocked by his words and half impressed I'm not babbling like an idiot. He looks confused.

"What are you talking about?"

Pulling out his phone, he looks at the screen before answering. "Yeah. Right here. My agent texted this morning. We're supposed to go on tour." I continue to stare at him. "I take it you know nothing about this."

I shake my head. This is bad. It's so, so bad. I can't go on tour with Spencer Garrison! I barely made it through the last signing when I saw him for all of five minutes total. Hours upon hours, days upon days, I'm likely to forget how to breathe completely. Or I'll barf on his shoe.

"I just found out about it today. I wouldn't normally agree to something like this, but it's right after the holidays, so I'm free. And they have us hitting a lot of the cities both the summer and winter X Games have been held in, so it sounds cool. Philly, Minneapolis, Austin, and then we head back to the West Coast. Your agent hasn't told you yet?"

"I've been offline today. I took the day off to try and push through my writer's block."

"By coming to Venice Beach?"

I shrug. "I was looking for some surfers."

He gets a strange look on his face before adding, "You're not from around here, are you?"

I shake my head, still stunned that I'm supposed to go on tour. With Spencer Garrison. How am I supposed to sleep with him in the room next to mine? There's no way.

Spencer runs his hand through his hair and smiles again. "You're never going to find the inspiration you're looking for here."

I hold myself back from snorting a laugh. Jokes on him. My muse showed up unexpectedly and currently I'm having all kinds of inspirational fantasies I will never tell him about.

"Zuma is where you need to be. And there's a great place to eat on the way there. Can I show you?"

As much as I want to say no and run away, I find myself nodding. I have clearly lost my mind if I'm agreeing to this but at this point, he's the only one with information about this alleged tour. Well, other than my publicist and once I get on the phone with her, I may never get off. Plus, I could eat. Besides, if history is any indication, I'm not going to win the battle against my agent about this tour. If I'm going to make it through, I probably need to learn how to breathe around him soon.

Then again, maybe passing out will get me a note from my doctor on why travel is a bad idea.

No, Aggi. You can do this.

My new book *and* fulfilling all my contractual obligations might just depend on it.

Chapter 10

"I thought you said we were going to eat on the way to Zuma?"

Smiling, I open the door to my favorite bar and grill on the boardwalk and motion for Adeline to enter first. She hesitates for only a second as she peers up at me through her dark lashes. I could tell she was nervous earlier, not unlike she was in Chicago, but right now standing in front of me, she looks slightly annoyed. I like it. Her. I like her.

"Hiya, how many?" the hostess asks as I step behind Adeline. "Two. A table on the patio if you have it, please . . . Natalie," I say, using the hostess's name with my big, mega-watt smile that the sponsors love in their ads.

Blushing, Natalie says, "Let me clear off a table for you."

Turning on her heel, Adeline looks up at me, but we're standing so close she has to crane her neck so far, and she stumbles a bit. Reaching out, I grab her before she hits the ground.

"Careful, Adi," I say with a chuckle as she rights herself and brushes hair from her face. Damn she's adorable. "It's okay if I call you Adi? I saw that your agent used that for your name on the email."

"What? Oh, my name. Of course. Why are we here again?"

"To eat?" I know what she means and I'm being a little ornery right now, but the way she contorts her face as she processes my simple answer is too amusing to stop.

She crosses her arms over her chest and I'm not sure if she's about to give me a tongue lashing or run away. I don't get the chance to find out though, because the hostess returns and offers to take us to our table. Adi turns but hesitates before moving. I place my hand on the small of her back to nudge her forward. The moment my hand touches her back, she lets out a small squeak before walking.

The tension is a little thicker than I'm used to as we both look over the menu. I don't know why I bother, I get the same thing each time I come here. A classic patty melt is my go-to order at any greasy spoon, but this place blows them all out of the water. When the server returns with our iced teas to take our order, I wait a few beats for Adi to speak. Instead, she looks out across the boardwalk, seemingly in thought.

Clearing my throat, I watch as she exhales, almost in resignation, as she turns her attention to me.

"I brought you here because this place is my go-to for a good burger. I only flew in this morning and went straight to physical therapy. I'm pretty sure I'm five minutes from my stomach eating itself. Plus, its great people watching. When we're done, we'll head up to Zuma and see if we can find you some inspiration for your story."

"Oh. Okay. Thanks." She chews on her lip for a second before quickly adding, "I'm starting to feel hangry, which is a real condition you know, so it's good. Eating is good. I like to eat."

Laughing at the cute blush that crosses her face, I take a drink from my glass as she finally offers me a full smile. This is different than the smile she had at the book event with her readers. That smile is beautiful, but this one, with her across from me with little to no makeup on and her hair unkempt from the ocean wind, is just more. It's like I'm seeing the real her, not the author her. It's a look I know well, because I do the same thing when interacting with fans. I bet Adeline Snow and I have a lot in common when it comes to our public persona versus our real self.

"So, this tour thing," I say leaning back in my chair.

Adi scrunches her face in response and mocks my position. "Sorry about that. I'm sure it was my publicist's idea. She's always trying to get me to do things that are "new" or "innovative." She uses air quotes and I laugh at the expression on her face. If Adeline Snow wanted to quit writing, professional poker player would not be a career option for her. The girl has no poker face.

"Nah, I'd put money on my agent. Freddy is determined to keep me in the spotlight as long as he can. Retirement is not his favorite word, and I've been throwing it around a lot lately."

Adi's eyes widen and she's about to say something when our server appears next to our table, but when she turns to the couple next to us, I watch her shoulders sag in disappointment. Laughing, I say, "Hungry?"

"It feels like my insides are feasting on themselves." I watch as she bites her lip like she's preventing herself from speaking.

"You bite any harder on your lip and it'll bleed. What's got you all in tangles?"

Sighing, she looks down and begins fiddling with the silverware. "I kind of wish I'd ordered a burger now." Laughing, I lean back in my chair as we engage in a little more small talk mostly about the pros and cons of hard shell tacos versus soft shell. Just as I'm proving my point on putting the hard shell in the soft, our server arrives with our food. My patty melt looks and smells amazing. Adi opted for the fish tacos and now I too am second guessing my food choice.

"I've got some major food envy over that plate, Adi."

"Ditto, Spencer."

We dig into our food while talking about everything and nothing. Well, I do most of the talking. It's clear she's still nervous around me, but she's starting to relax. Thankfully we seem to get along because the next few weeks are going to be crazy, and if she hated me that'd kind of suck.

"Wait. You hate social media?" I ask when she mentions having an aversion to Instagram. "Isn't that a huge part of your job? My sister went on and on about your online stuff. Full disclosure, Kate is a bit of a stalker when it comes to you. And, shit I hate saying this but . . ." Adi stops with her taco almost to her mouth and raises a brow in question before I continue. "She's kind of responsible for all of this. She's the one who posted those pictures originally. Her heart was in a good place, she just didn't think of the shitstorm that would follow. To my sister I'm just her annoying little brother, not a 'celebrity'."

Instead of responding immediately, Adi takes a small bite of her taco then places it back on the plate before wiping her mouth with her napkin and taking a long drink from her iced tea. Crap, she's pissed.

"I do hate social media, but it's part of the job. I try to limit my time online to just a few pop ins each day. Hence my antiquated phone." She waves an old school flip phone at me briefly before dropping it back down on the table. "I like comments or photos I'm tagged in and deal with my in boxes when I log in. Otherwise, I avoid it at all costs. Being 'on'," she says with air quotes again, "is fucking exhausting. Plus the drama makes me queasy."

"I hear ya. Nobody told me when I was eight that being good at a sport was going to mean I have to spend half my life on my phone tapping a little blue thumb or a heart."

"Your sister was very sweet, and I could see how much she loves you. I think it's great she forgets your celebrity status. Besides, it was a great picture."

Yeah it was, but the one I sent to myself was better. Adeline uninhibited and not posing. Just her in a moment. Joy in her expression and an obvious love for what she does shining through. It makes me wonder where she got her creativity from.

"Do you have any siblings?"

She takes a moment to swallow her bite before answering. "Only child. But I was practically raised with my best friend so it never felt that way."

"Were you raised on a commune or something?" I chuckle before realizing she might have been. The smile drops off my face as I wonder if I just stuck my foot in my mouth. "Wait. Were you?"

"Raised on a commune?" When I nod, probably looking as pale as I feel, a smile crosses her face. "No. But my childhood was not what you'd call, conventional." She wipes her hands on a napkin and leans into the table, eyes looking off like she's remembering. "Do you watch the *Big Bang Theory*?"

The question throws me off. I'm not sure what this has to do with the topic at hand, but I just go with it. "I love that show."

"Me, too. You know Leonard's mom? She's like a neuroscientist or something."

"Uh huh."

"That's basically my mom."

I freeze mid-bite. "Really?"

"Really. She's loving and supportive and kind. But she's not really . . . I don't know how to describe it. She doesn't really understand emotions all that much. No, that's wrong. She understands them, she's just genius level smart and doesn't connect the same way your stereotypical mom does."

I think about what she's telling me and how Adeline doesn't always seem comfortable around people. It makes sense if her mom doesn't do emotions the same way mine does.

"My best friend's mom, Jan, though, she was all about hugs and kisses and making cookies with us," she continues. "It was nice having both of them because they did such different things. Like, when we decided to build our first ramp, Jan stocked up on Band-Aids and bought us helmets, while my mom double checked the schematics and made sure we had the right sized screws so it wouldn't collapse on us."

"Sounds like a more balanced childhood than most of us had," I say, laughing as I lean back in the chair, relaxing as she continues her story.

"It really was. I got the best of both worlds. Made Christmas cookies and wrote letters to Santa with one, made volcanos for the science fair and got help with math homework from the other."

"So I guess you got your creativity from your dad then?"

She shrugs as she takes another nibble. "I don't know. I think the sperm donor must have been artistic in some way for me to be like I am."

I cringe. In the early days of their divorce, that's what my mom used to call my dad. She doesn't anymore, but I remember the anti-term of endearment.

"Sperm donor? Sounds like they had as bad of a break-up as my folks did." I pick up my sandwich, bringing to my mouth as she responds.

"Oh. No. My mom wanted a baby but didn't want to mess with a relationship. He really is a sperm donor. Number four-seventeen in the book of choices."

I immediately choke on my sandwich, shocked by her admission. The nonchalant way she mentions her mom using a sperm bank to have her is not at all what I expected.

"Are you okay?"

Holding my finger up indicating I need a minute, I clear my throat as quickly as possible. Seriously. Can this woman shock me even more?

Finally I'm able to pull myself back together. "Sorry. You surprised me, that's all."

A blush crosses her face. "Yeah, maybe I shouldn't have said that. This is why I don't talk about my family very much."

"No," I say quickly. "No, please don't be embarrassed. I think it's really interesting. Unique. Somehow it fits you. I can't imagine you having a traditional childhood. That seems too bland for you somehow."

She clears her throat and sits back. It's clear that despite my attempt at a compliment, the roll she was on is over. "Moving on to a different topic, you mentioned retirement earlier. As a fan of your sport I'm kind of freaking out."

Sitting back, I humor her and contemplate how to best respond. I'm not dead set on giving up my career yet, but I'm close. "I'm not twenty anymore. My body is beat to hell. Every morning, it takes me at least ten minutes to roll out of bed because a different part of my body aches. I am currently recovering from my second knee surgery. Which, by the way, if my doctor or physical therapists knew I was on a board today they would kill me. So mum's the word, okay?"

She narrows her eyes playfully. "You do know there were half a dozen people at the park today who saw you, right?"

"Oh before you got there, I made them all swear on their boards they'd keep quiet. They were just stoked for some coaching."

Taking a large bite from my burger, I chew while she peppers me with a few more questions about retirement.

"You've heard of my non-profit?" She nods. "I want to dedicate more time to that. Building these parks and establishing alternatives for kids other than sitting around playing video games and wasting their youth away is important to me. I was lucky to be good at something at a young age and build a career out of it, but I want to do more. I have the means so why not do it now while I can still enjoy it?"

"Wow. That's amazing. I feel the same way," she says, a starry-eyed look crossing her face.

"How so?"

"I want to do more than just write books. Don't get me wrong, I love what I do. It's my dream, and I'm so lucky to be what we in the industry call a hybrid.

I have a publisher I'm committed to, but I still write and publish independently as an indie author. It's the best of both worlds, but I'm always chasing a deadline and sometimes I lose the joy of writing by the time I finish a book. And there's always another deadline just ahead. I'd like to do more. To give back somehow."

"Well, Adeline Snow, it sounds like this impromptu pairing may be beneficial for us both. We have an opportunity to talk to people about the things we are passionate about."

Smiling, Adi nods her head vigorously before turning her attention back to her taco. We continue talking as we finish our meal and by the time the server returns to clear our table, the sun is setting in the distance, and I look at my phone for the time.

"Tell me why people care about coffee." Adi's focus is in her purse, but she quickly turns to look at me, confusion written all over her face. "My assistant just text me that she's put reminders in my calendar for me to take pictures of my coffee. This is why I hate social media. Nobody should care how I have my coffee or whether or not I like the yellow jelly beans. It's ridiculous."

"Do you?" She asks as she holds her credit card out for me, but I wave it off as I put my own card in the ticket holder for the server.

"Do I what?"

"Eat the yellow jelly beans. You can tell a lot about a person by their jelly bean choices. Maybe that's why they care?"

I can't tell if she's teasing me or serious. Maybe poker would be a good alternative career choice for her.

"I don't discriminate when it comes to sugar."

"Good man. Why leave a poor jelly bean to suffer alone just because it's yellow? That'd be sad."

We're laughing at her statement when the server returns for me to sign the receipt. As we're walking out the door, Adi stops and it's easy to see the nerves she had earlier return. I thought we were past this, but I guess not.

"We should exchange numbers," I suggest.

"What? Why?" she stammers, and it's fucking adorable. Yep, nervous Adi is my favorite.

"Well, I think we're friends now and I like to have my friends' numbers. Plus, we both know we're going to need an ally when we deal with our publicists. And since we're going on tour together . . ."

She gulps. Loudly. "Oh. Yeah. I suppose."

I hand her my phone and she stares at it in her hand. "Text yourself with my phone. You'll have my number and I'll have yours."

Once I hear a little beep in her purse, I take my phone back from her and tap her name into the contacts as she does the same, though it takes her much longer with that ancient phone. A small smirk appears on her face and for the briefest moment, I feel like the dude in her books.

"Let me walk you to your car. We'll try Zuma tomorrow."

Without hesitation, Adi turns and begins walking down the boardwalk. I follow her and have a feeling this is the beginning of a very fun friendship.

Chapter 11

Aggi

First Stop: Philadelphia
Home of Summer X Games circa 2001 and 2002

We never did make it to Zuma. Not because Spencer didn't try. Oh, he texted all right. I just didn't respond. Instead, I fixated on the fact that I had shared so much personal information and let my nerves take over. Then I allowed myself to succumb to the belief that if I ignore the upcoming tour, it'll go away.

Obviously, my spirit animal is an ostrich. Stick your head in the sand and nothing bad can happen, right?

Wrong. The tour didn't go away. Over the next few months, my publicist and Spencer's publicist worked together to get everything finalized. Despite my dread, and maybe a few ugly comments which my team ignored, an itinerary showed up in my email last week. It freaked me out so much, I skimmed it and caught the important parts:

Three weeks. Six cites. Spencer Garrison and I.

Alone.

Well, not totally alone. The general public will be around. And as always, we've be assigned a point of contact at each signing to make sure we're where we need to be and when.

But yes, we'll be traveling together by ourselves. Sitting next to each other on six airplanes. Sleeping next door to each other in six hotels. Standing next to each other at six signings. It is both my dream and my nightmare come true.

My dream because all six cities are locations where the X Games have been held. It's an extreme sports lover's fantasy vacation.

But mostly it's my nightmare because I feel like I'm going to throw up all the Christmas turkey I ate over the holidays as I drown in my denial. All the deep breathing exercises I did on the two-and-a-half-hour flight to begin this tour didn't calm my nerves. However, I have a large collection of barf bags stuffed in my carry-on, courtesy of the flight attendant that thought for sure I wasn't going to make it.

Exiting the plane, I swing into the restroom to do my business and a quick touch-up of my makeup. Unbeknownst to me, because I always forget to check, my flight was delayed long enough that I have to go straight to our first signing. No checking in at the hotel. No deep breathing exercises in my room to try and become Zen and one with my inner yogi. No anxiety eating from the minibar. Nope. I had to transform at the airport and take the entire plane ride complete in Adeline Snow makeup and dress. Except for my heels. For good reasons, they are in my carry-on. No way I was trucking through an airport in anything higher than my bright teal Converse. That's just asking for me to get my heel stuck on the bottom of an escalator and I have no desire to channel Buddy the Elf.

Satisfied that Adeline Snow is firmly in place, I roll my suitcase into the terminal and toward baggage claim. I hate having two suitcases. I try really hard to pack lighter than that. But January means winter clothes up north and possibly shorts down south. Not to mention, I have no idea if I'll have laundry facilities for the next three weeks. I don't have that many pairs of underwear. I may have to hit up a local VS to buy more if I run out.

I find my baggage claim and walk that direction when a tall man catches my eye.

No. No it can't be. I thought I had another hour to prepare myself!

But no. Fate is a cruel, cruel bitch and Spencer Garrison is standing right by the carousel while I'm thinking about my undergarments.

Pull yourself together, Aggi. He's just a man. A very talented, very sexy man, who is LOOKING RIGHT AT YOU OHMYGOD!!

Somehow, I stumble over the wheel of my suitcase when he smiles my direction. No idea how that is even possible since the bag is behind me, but I don't have time to figure it out. Spencer Garrison is walking my way and I have about four seconds to get my heart to stop pounding so hard and breathe again . . .

Three . . . two . . . one . . .

"Hi."

Looking up into his deep blues, it's a miracle in and of itself that I haven't passed out, fallen over, or thrown up on his shoe. So far, so good.

"Wha-what are you doing here?"

Hey look at that! A coherent sentence! I mentally pat myself on the back. But not too hard. Wouldn't want to jinx myself.

He shoves his phone in the back pocket of his very nice fitting jeans. "My flight got here about twenty minutes ago, so I figured we could ride together to the event. I hope that wasn't too presumptuous of me." I watch him carefully as he pulls his phone back from his pocket and then places it back again. It's like he doesn't know what to do with his hands.

Wait . . . is he . . . nervous?

"Are you nervous?"

Crap. I wasn't supposed to say that out loud. Fortunately, he doesn't seem to be fazed by it. Instead, a slight blush creeps across his tan cheeks and he runs his fingers through his lush dirty blond hair.

"A little."

"But . . . why?"

I'm honestly stumped. Spencer Garrison balances on a skateboard in front of millions of people on a regular basis. I can't walk in front of ten people without falling over. Spencer Garrison models in his underwear in ads targeted to the masses. I hide my true self behind makeup and a persona. Spencer Garrison is beautiful and well spoken. I'm neither of those things. What in the world does he have to be nervous about?

I watch as he bites his bottom lip. Vaguely, I notice my own nerves slip away as I focus on him.

"The only book signing I've ever been to was the one with my sister. I don't really know what's going to happen."

"Oh." I find myself a little disappointed in his answer, but not quite sure why. "Is that it? There aren't going to be nearly as many people at these signings as there were at your last games. It should be no biggie for you."

"Yeah, but I don't really talk to people at the games. I'm skating, Sure, I do interviews with magazines and stuff, but those reporters tend to ask questions about the sport, which I'm comfortable with. This one-on-one stuff is very different. Plus"—he scratches the back of his neck—"I kind of like you, and I'm a little nervous I'll say the wrong thing."

My jaw practically hits the ground and it takes a solid ten seconds to realize it. "I . . . uh . . . what?"

"I thought we had a good time in California, but when you didn't text me back I started to second guess myself and . . . you know what? Never mind."

I don't know how to respond to that, so I don't. Instead, we stand awkwardly in silence as I go through my mental list of conversation starting topics before coming up with an appropriate question. "So how were the holidays?"

"Good, good," he says quickly. "Got to see my sister."

"Oh, how is she?"

"She's good." He shoves his hands in his pockets and there's the awkward pause again. Just as I open my mouth to ask another question, he beats me to is. "Do you see your bag on the carousel?"

I look over at the suitcases moving by but don't really see much of anything. I'm still stuck on the fact that Spencer Garrison *likes me* and can't seem to put together a coherent thought any more than I can. I look over my shoulder trying to catch a glimpse of Ashton Kutcher because surely I'm being Punk'd right now.

Nope. No celebrity sighting.

My emotions are suddenly at war with each other. My dream guy, the guy I've been crushing on from afar likes me. Part of me is ecstatic at this news. Another part of me is terrified. What if he only likes *Adeline Snow*, not Agnes Sylvester. There's a difference.

Still a third part of me is mad about this turn of events. I can't date my muse. I need him to continue inspiring me and giving me fantasies and plot twists I can weave into stories for my fans. I have a contract to fulfill and a career I've committed my life to. I can't mess that up by taking the one thing that has inspired me over the years and making him "human."

Can I?

"Adeline?"

"What?" My eyes snap up to his, even as my thoughts continue to swirl.

"Your suitcase."

"Oh." A slight shake of my head clears the fog out of my brain. "Yeah. My suitcase. Um . . . it's that one right there. With all the bumper stickers."

He smirks when he sees it. Admittedly it's hard not to miss. Every time I travel somewhere, I get a bumper sticker and put it on the hard plastic. It's my little reminder of all the things I've done and all the places I've gone. Makes me feel like I'm getting out in the world and living life. Plus, it makes it so much easier to find at the airport.

Grabbing it from the carousel, Spencer's bicep bulges and I find myself questioning my own insecurities. I wouldn't mind having that arm wrapped around me.

No, no, no! He's your muse. Plus, it's too soon. You've gone to dinner once. Your one and only goal tonight is to make it through the signing without throwing up or end up looking like an idiot on social media again. Stay focused.

"Thank you," I say shyly and attempt to take it from him, but he doesn't let go.

"If it's okay with you, I already scheduled an Uber to take us to the bookstore."

I nod, probably a little too vigorously and respond with, "Yeah. That's great. Thank you."

We walk silently to the door marked "passenger pick up" and quickly find the waiting car. Thankfully, we seem to have gotten a chivalrous driver. He quickly ushers us into the car and puts our suitcases in the trunk. I'm grateful he doesn't make me stand in the cold. Chilly temps don't bother me, but the wind practically goes right through me, and I really don't want to shave my legs again tonight, although it is winter in the northeast, so it's probably inevitable. No one wants to have prickly legs when wearing a dress, and that's what I packed. Clearly I didn't think about temperatures when I threw everything in a suitcase.

The twenty-minute drive crawls by as none of us talk. I try desperately to come up with something to say, some conversation starter, but I'm stumped. It doesn't help that Spencer's scent practically surrounds me, making my knees weak. Thank goodness for small victories like not having to stand up.

When we finally arrive at the store, I can see people through the giant glass windows already sitting, waiting for us. I close my eyes and take a deep breath, centering myself and forcing Adeline Snow to come to the surface. Our lovely driver, who only broke a few laws getting us here on time, opens my car door and smiles kindly at me.

"Have a good evening," he says before disappearing into his car, leaving Spencer and me alone on the sidewalk with our luggage.

"Well. Are *you* ready for this?"

"I'm never completely ready," I admit. "But it's part of the job. Are you ready?"

I watch as all the anxiety he's been sporting fades away and the confident, charming Spencer Garrison reappears. *How does he do that so easily?*

Suddenly the front door flies open and a short brunette comes barreling out the door. "Oh good! You're here!" Her curly hair is flying around in the wind so her face is barely visible. Somehow, she can see through it all, and she grabs the handle of Spencer's suitcase. "Come with me. I'll take you to the employee breakroom so you can get ready."

She takes off through the door and Spencer and I have to race to catch up. Ducking our heads, we both avoid eye contact with anyone who may recognize us, although it's hard not to notice the woman dragging suitcases noisily through the store followed by an amazing looking man who somehow makes traveling look glamourous. The crowd begins to murmur and I'm sure I see a flash from a camera or two. Fingers crossed I don't accidentally see stars and run into something.

"Phew!" the crazy haired lady says after we, and all of our luggage, make it behind a door marked "employees only." "Sorry to whisk you through the store so quickly. Several super fans have been here all day. I was afraid they'd see you and we'd never get them to leave you alone long enough to get back here."

Spencer's face blanches and I giggle/snort at how out of his element he really is. You would think being in the public eye he would be used to this, but I suppose book nerds are a breed all their own.

"Anyway, I'm Amy," she continues excitedly. "I'll be your assistant tonight and will make sure you get to your hotel after we're done. We still have about ten minutes before the signing is supposed to start. Are you hungry? Do you need anything?"

"Just a restroom if you have one," Spencer says.

"Of course!" She leads him around the corner, leaving me alone with my thoughts. Grabbing my heels from my bag, I'm stuck on how different this Spencer is. Is he not as confident as he seems to be? It wouldn't necessarily be a huge stretch. Lots of celebrities put on a show. It's just one more layer to him I'm seeing.

The next little while is a blur. When we're ready, Amy ushers us to a table in the middle of the store amidst cheers and squeals of delight. There are several dozen chairs filled with readers and tagalongs. Probably a few husbands who have come for moral support. Dozens of people stand in the back. Fortunately, Amy has a microphone set up.

After a brief introduction, she hands me the floor. Taking the microphone, I fall back on the intro I usually give.

"Hi everyone. My name is Adeline Snow, and this is Spencer Garrison. We're so happy to be here tonight."

I pause and smile at the crowd, giving myself a second to make sure I'm still breathing.

"I think it's safe to say if you're here, you're familiar with my *Extreme Love* Series." A few ladies applaud while one shouts a very enthusiastic "seven times" from the back of the room. Well okay then. "That makes me so happy. This series is very near and dear to my heart. My latest release, Freestyle, is a project I'm very proud of. Who knew what kind of sparks would come alive when two competitive snowboarders met in an airport? Anyway, my next release in this series is still under wraps but I promise it will fall right in line with everything you expect from this series." It better. If I ever write it.

"Many of you probably recognize my co-host, Spencer Garrison, from his many appearances in the X Games. How many golds do you have, Spencer? Five?" I ask as he nods in response. I've not spent a lot of time with Spencer, but I can tell by the look on his face, he's either ready to bolt or throw up. I get it, I really do. I'm honestly surprised I'm as calm as I am right now. I'm both pleasantly surprised with myself and waiting for the inevitable "Aggi moment" to happen.

"Well, as you know my series is centered around the X Games, and who better to spend a time with me while I visit a few of the cities that have held our beloved games other than him." The men in the crowd seem to like this tidbit and visibly relax when they realize this isn't an event only for women.

"I've rambled enough, so let's make it easy and open the floor to questions for either of us."

I point at the first hand that goes up, although I can't see who it is until she stands. A red-faced, red haired woman looks delighted to be here, which makes me happy. I love when readers are happy.

"Hi Adeline. I've read all your books."

Another thing to smile about. "Thank you."

"But I notice in this series the main male characters always have dirty blond hair and blue eyes. Is there any reason for that? Is that your type, personally?"

Glancing at Spencer, I notice a strange look on his

face. Quickly turning away, I pray my face isn't red. That's a dead giveaway that my *type* is sitting right next to me.

Also, I make a mental note to search my next book and make sure the hero has black hair and brown eyes. "I don't really have one," I lie. "Just lots of stories in my head."

The crowd murmurs, and they probably don't believe me, but at least it's done. I lied through my teeth and am hopefully moving on. But that look on Spencer's face has me spooked. It's like he could see right through me.

I just hope he didn't see anything he didn't like.

Chapter 12

Spencer

I lied. A lot. I'm not nervous about this signing at all. Crowds don't bother me in the slightest, and I really don't care what people think of me. But I care what Adeline thinks. I care way too much.

She's quirky and beautiful but she's so much more. She's talented. I've been reading her books like it's my job and now I get it. Her words are a thing of magic. There are dips and turns and flips. It's like skateboarding but with words on a page.

Beyond all of that, she's kind and patient. Even in Chicago, anyone could see she gets a little shy and would prefer not to have the spotlight on her. But, with her fans she's amazing. She is engaged, and her smile never looks forced or fake. Well, except when we took a picture together.

I've been around my fair share of celebrities, both in the entertainment and sports industries, and it's not often I encounter someone who seems to have a true and honest affection for their fans. So many take the "little people" for granted. But not Adeline Snow. She sees them, and she connects with them.

It's strange to me that at both book related events I've been to, Adeline has been a speaker and the question of her muse has come up. She seems to skirt the question and wave it off like it's unimportant. If people are asking, surely it is important to them. Truthfully, it's been a question I've had as well. After reading two of her books, I found a common theme with the lead characters. Specifically, the male characters. Kate told me to refer to them as the "Heroes," but I feel like a tool using that term, so I don't. Tonight, when the woman asked her what her type was, and described him, I watched her as she contemplated a response. Shouldn't that be a simple question? When she was asked if that was her type as well, I sat up a little straighter, curious myself. Tall, dark hair, and light eyes with an athletic build. I check all those boxes. If she's writing about them, maybe that's her type too.

I should be so lucky. What are the chances the attraction and connection I feel for Adeline is mutual? After the way she left me hanging in LA and again at the airport, I doubt it's true, but it would be nice.

Adi and I both answered questions for about thirty minutes. Okay, she did most of the answering while I smiled and nodded. I could have said more, but I was too engaged in watching her in her element. Her passion for her fans is a thing of beauty to me. I could have watched her all night.

Instead, after a brief intermission, we were directed to a small corner where a table was set up with two seats for us. Adi would be signing books and I would be, well I guess ready to take photos and meet and greet the three people who even know who I am here.

The line is long, but the organizers have given people numbers to allow them an opportunity to shop while they wait for their designated group to meet Adi. A few small clusters of people are lingering nearby and every so often I hear my name mentioned but mostly it's white noise as I play out the time I've spent with Adeline Snow. Watching her at the conference, in the hallway when I stopped her, my sister and her ridiculous fangirl freak-outs. I smile as I think of how adorable she was slamming the door in the poor porter's face at the hotel and how she was so in the moment taking pictures at Venice Beach.

The look on her face when I basically told her I liked her keeps flashing through my mind like a damn strobe light. Was I too bold? Too forward? I was only being honest, and I thought she'd appreciate the honesty. The women she writes in her books are take charge and independent women. I thought for sure some of that was her. I mean, they also stumble and spill a lot. Surely, she wouldn't only write the silly things she does into her characters. Did I scare her away? Is she not interested at all? I thought we hit it off in Venice, but not getting a response to my texts certainly knocked my confidence level down a few pegs.

"Spencer?" Her hand on my bicep jars me from my thoughts. "Would you mind taking a picture? Lisa's son is a huge fan of yours and she'd love to get a picture with you too." I look up at the woman standing before us. Her smile is huge and she's bouncing a little on her toes.

"Of course. I have a few of these photos," I say, motioning to the pile of glossies Freddy shipped to the bookstore. I forgot he told me about them until one of the employees dropped them off at our table. "Would your son like one autographed?"

You'd think I offered Lisa the key to my new house in Lexington the way she squeals. Okay then. "What's his name?"

"Cayden. That's C-A-Y-D-E-N. Oh, my goodness. Thank you. He's going to flip."

I quickly scribble a note to Cayden and sign my name before handing a few pictures to Lisa and rising from my seat. Lisa and Adi have shifted a little and there's nowhere for me to stand so I walk around the table instead, not knowing where to stand.

"Oh Adi, would you mind if Spencer is in the middle?"

Adi smiles and I kind of fumble a little, surprised one of her fans would want to stand next to me. Lisa snuggles in close but not Adi. She's at least two full steps away from us.

Needing to be closer to her, I take a chance and grab her around the waist. Immediately she tenses, but I don't get the feeling it's from being uncomfortable. It's more like her anxiety has kicked in again.

Wanting to help, I lean in and whisper, "Relax. We're just taking pictures."

She continues to fidget so I try another tactic using my modeling 101 training.

"Smile."

She stops fidgeting momentarily but is still frozen. Glancing at her face, I suppress a chuckle.

"Stop flaring your nostrils," I whisper.

Her shoulders suddenly relax, but it's painfully obvious she doesn't know what to do in this position.

"Put your hand on your hip."

She raises her arm and . . .

"Oof." I suck in a breath and try desperately not to topple over as pain shoots through my abdomen. "Wrong arm."

"Ohmygod." Her hands fly over her face. "I just elbowed you in the junk, didn't I? Ohmygod."

People in the crowd begin to snicker and I know this moment in time is about to go viral.

Again.

•••

Other than the punch to the junk, the rest of the night went by quickly. The store had this type of event down to a science and although it's late here, I'm still on California time. My stomach rumbles and reminds me it's been hours since I've had so much as a piece of cheese.

"Sorry, I didn't realize how hungry I was."

Adi smiles at me shyly, clearly worn out from peopling. "Don't worry, I'm sure my stomach will join the chorus soon enough."

Laughing, I stretch my legs out and habitually rub my knee a little as I twist my leg. Thankfully, the car that picked us up was a large town car. I'm sure I have Freddy to thank for that. Or not, considering the last time he was in charge of setting up my car service, he forgot to tell them how tall I was, and I ended up riding in the Prius version of a clown car.

"How about we stop for some dinner?"

Adi hesitates, and I can see an excuse forming in her cute little mind. "Adi, we're both starving, even though I'm on LA time, it's late here. What would you say to splitting a pizza and a pitcher of beer?"

Her stomach answers for her, and I lean forward to tell the driver to take us to the best pizza place in town when her phone rings. She grumbles under her breath and ignores the call. And it rings again.

"Sounds like it's important."

"Not likely," she mumbles as she taps the answer button and brings the phone to her ear.

"Can I call you back?" It's not a greeting of hello or even a casual hi so I assume it's personal and not her agent.

"I said can I call you back. Oh, dear Lord." Taking a huge breath and exhaling dramatically, she looks my way and says, "Sorry about this."

I'm about to question her when she pulls the phone down and taps the speaker button.

"Can you hear me now?"

"What is this a Verizon commercial?" A deep male voice asks on the other end of the line. Is it her boyfriend? Maybe that explains her hesitation around me.

She rolls her eyes. "I had to put you on speaker. I don't know what's wrong with my phone. For some reason it's automatically muting me."

"Did you spill water on it?"

"No."

"Dr. Pepper?"

Her face flushes. "Shut up, Todd."

He laughs through the phone. "Oh my dear Agnes. You're so predictable."

Agnes? Why did he call her Agnes? I look at her questioningly, but she pretends I'm not there as she taps her fingers quickly on her leg and glances to me with wide eyes. I'm not sure what the look is for, but I find it endearing. Her mouth opens and closes like she's going to say something but instead she pulls her top lip between her teeth and her brows furrow. It's cute as hell and I slowly smile in response. Her eyes widen again but this time, it's not a look of horror or nervousness, it's surprise. She inhales quickly, her breath making a swoosh sound as her eyes glance to my mouth and then back to my eyes.

It's a simple look and only a few seconds, but it feels like everything just shifted between us. And I like it. I like the way she looks at me. For the first time in a long time, it makes me feel like I'm more than just a skater. Which could be problematic since she's talking to some guy.

"Aggi? Are you there? Oh Jesus, did you fall or something?" The voice on the phone is shouting and banging something but Adi, or Aggi, is still looking at me.

"Todd, I'll call you later." She disconnects the phone and tosses it in her purse before leaning her head back and rubbing her hands down her face.

"So, Agnes?"

"Ugh."

I break out in laughter at her response just as the car pulls up in front of a small pizza joint.

"Let's go grab some grub," I say, opening the door and turning to extend my hand to her. She hesitates for a second but then places her small hand in my large one and lets me help her out of the car. And it's for naught because she still stumbles, releases a few curses, and then makes her way into the restaurant.

Oh, yeah. I like this girl.

A large pizza with the works and a pitcher of beer sit between us on the table, the topic of Agnes not even remotely broached. That's mostly because both of our agents and publicists have been texting or calling us. They're far too excited for the response tonight and apparently our social media presence is "killer" according to Freddy. Great.

"I hate social media," she grumbles as she tops off both of our pints.

"I hear ya. I say we ignore them the rest of the night and enjoy this pie before it gets too cold and this beer gets warm."

After a few bites and a signal to the server for another pitcher of beer, I sit back in my seat. Lifting my glass to my lips, I pause and ask, "So, are we talking about it?"

"I'd rather not."

"I'm assuming Adeline Snow isn't your real name?"

She crinkles her nose like she doesn't want to answer, but knows she's been found out. "It's not. Well, it's my professional name. My pen name. So technically, it's kind of my name."

"But not your real name. Not the one that goes with the real you." It's a statement not a question. I already knew there were two versions of this woman, I just didn't know there were two names. Two complete personas.

"Ugh, I could kill Todd."

"Is Todd your boyfriend?" Please say no.

By the hard grimace she flashes my way, it's a pretty safe bet that I just assumed and almost made an "ass out of you and me." "Ew. No. That's my . . . Todd. I mean . . . Todd. Just Todd is his name. No, not 'just Todd.' His name is Todd." She pauses to take a deep breath and probably to center herself. I can't help being amused. "Todd is my best friend. The one I told you I watched the X Games with? He's so not my boyfriend. Even thinking about him that way makes me want to bleach my brain."

That earns a chuckle from me. "Okay, not your boyfriend. That's good."

"It is? I mean, it is. That'd be gross. I know that, but you don't."

"It's good for me. I'd hate for you to have a boy-friend."

She chokes a little on her beer at my statement, so I continue. "I like your name."

Her eyes widen, and she takes another sip from her beer before tilting her head. She's assessing me. Trying to figure out if I'm teasing or serious.

"Nobody likes my name. Well, except my grand-mother. She loved it."

"I think it fits you. Agnes . . . is Snow your last name?" Shaking her head, I wait for her to provide her name. When she isn't forthcoming, I motion with my hand as I take a bite of pizza for her to continue.

She sighs deeply like she's done trying to keep up with the pretense. "Well, you already know so what's the harm, I suppose? It's Sylvester. My name is Agnes Sylvester. Clearly not a name that's going to sell ro-mance books. Hence the pen name."

"What do your friends call you?"

"Aggi. It's why I went with Adeline and go by Adi. It's close enough when I'm jumping into Adi mode. Having two names can get confusing."

"I can see that. Well, Aggi," I say, eliciting a raised eyebrow from her as I raise my glass to toast. "I'm looking forward to getting to know you. I think this is the beginning of a long and beautiful relationship."

"Friendship."

"If you say so," I answer, and we clink our glasses together.

Chapter 13

Aggi

There is not enough concealer in this world to help with the six-piece luggage set I'm carrying under my eyes. Bags for days. Who does Spencer Garrison think he is, telling me he's glad I don't have a boyfriend? Calling our friendship a relationship. What alternate universe is he living in? And he likes my name?

I wasn't kidding when I said nobody liked my name. It's a family name and while I love my family and my grandmother, my name kind of sucks.

I shouldn't have drunk all those beers because I started to believe him. The way he looked at me, the way he smiled at me, and the way everything made me feel. Like it could be real. He could mean it all.

Fucking Todd. I swear I'm going to kill him. Later. I'm not exactly sure what for, but right now it's easier to place blame on him than on myself, so there you have it. Besides, I don't have time to do it now.

I'm running late to meet Spencer in the lobby. Our flight leaves in two hours and although we aren't too far from the airport, traffic is rarely on my side.

Plus, there's always my faithful nemesis, security. For some reason, no matter how many prayers I send up, I always get stopped so they can rub their swabs and wipes on my laptop. I told the last TSA guy it was the sugar from my donuts on the keys. He didn't care, and I was almost late for my flight.

I quickly gather my things and speed walk out of my room and down the hall to the elevators. Glancing at the large mirrors blanketing the elevator, I cringe at my appearance. It's not pretty. Oh well, Spencer wanted to know me. Today is a travel day and I'm travel ready. I'm decked out in my preferred travel outfit— leggings, a flowy tank, and a cardigan with my hair piled high on my head in a loose bun and other than the efforts to hide the circles, my makeup is minimal, and my glasses are on. There is no better concealer than the thick black rims. Plus, the idea of contacts make me want to poke my eye out. And frankly, with as tired as I am, actually poking my eye out would have been likely.

Stepping out of the elevator I walk quickly around the corner dragging my suitcases behind me and—

"Oof!"

"Whoa, slow down there speedster." Spencer's arms are around me after barreling into him, with no indication he's going to let me go.

I take a moment to breath him in—*I mean* center myself—before pulling away.

"Sorry. I know we're late for the airport."

He flashes that megawatt smile and I find myself

wanting to breathe him in again. *Down girl!*

"It's okay. I already checked us in and we are TSA PreCheck, so security won't take that long."

I'm both excited and stunned that we won't be late. Excited because I probably won't have to run through the airport. That's more dangerous than lighting a cigarette on a plane. And stunned because I've never been lucky enough to get TSA PreCheck. Maybe travelling with Spencer will be easier than I thought.

"Our Uber is waiting, though," he continues as he grabs the handle of my larger suitcase, leaving me with the carry-on.

Following close behind, the chill from the wind goes right through my clothes straight into my bones. Or at least that's how it feels. I'm so glad we're doing the coldest legs of our trip first.

Climbing into the Uber, we settle ourselves in for a short ride. Thankfully, we're only about twenty minutes from the airport. It's still making me anxious to cut it so close, but traffic seems light. Besides, what's the worst that can happen? We miss our flight and I have to spend more time with Spencer at the airport, that's what.

And I don't have time to try and bang out another chapter.

And we're potentially late for our next signing.

And our publicists could end up having a ton of pissed off people on their hands that they have to deal with, making them cranky which in turn makes me flustered—okay yeah, we need this Uber to move faster.

"I like the glasses."

Forgetting what my spiraling thoughts were about, I turn to look at Spencer. This is twice in the last twelve hours he's said he likes something that makes me insecure about myself. I don't understand what's happening here. "Really?"

"Yeah. They make you look, I don't know . . . real."

I blink. "Real?"

"Yeah. Like I'm getting to see the real you. Not the persona you want everyone else to see."

I blink rapidly as my mouth opens to respond, but I can't think of one thing to say. It's like he cracked the very fragile shell I have carefully built up around me, so he can taste the chocolate on the inside.

Also, I make a mental note to never try to use M&M as an analogy because that didn't quite work as well as I thought it would.

Either way, I'm a bit flabbergasted, so instead of saying anything, I sit quietly, letting my mind wander to our next stop—Minneapolis. I've never been to the Twin Cities, but I know The Garrison Foundation has a facility there. Not that I've been stalking the list of locations or anything, I'm just knowledgeable about charitable organizations I respect. Plus, Minneapolis is home to the 2017 X Games and those were the last games Spencer competed in. I can see now how his being on this tour with me makes sense. I settle into my seat and let my mind wander.

By the time we make it to the airport, it's clear we don't have time to waste. With less than thirty minutes until boarding and no telling how far away our gate is, we both shuffle and shift anxiously as we wait in line to drop off our bags. And then wait again for the TSA agent to look over our IDs and boarding passes.

Finally, we catch a break and get the short security line, thanks to Spencer's magical check-in powers, which means no taking our shoes off. No pulling our electronics out. And for me, no gun powder residue check. Score!

Grabbing my bag, I race to the monitors to triple check our gate number, knowing Spencer is just two steps behind me.

"Oh no. Spencer, we have to go to a different terminal." Looking over at him, he's not there. "Spencer?" I say swiveling around trying to find him. Finally, I home in on him and I can't help the laugh that comes out of my mouth.

He's being more thoroughly checked by security.

So much for me getting his good luck. Instead, he got my bad luck.

Sauntering back over, I wait as patiently as I can for him to get done. When Spencer finally gets the go ahead to leave, he just zips his duffle and grabs several items off the table, racing to me.

"Sorry about that. Where do we go?"

"We came in at the wrong terminal. We have to grab the shuttle. It's this way." Grabbing a few of the books out of his hand that he's about to drop, we make our way toward the marked entrance. It's only when we take a seat that I look down at the books in my hand

and realize . . .

These are all Adeline Snow books.

I quickly look up at him, knowing the questions are written all over my face. Questions I want to ask but am kind of afraid of knowing the answers to. As if he can sense my hesitation, he clears his throat and explains without me saying a word.

"Someone at the signing said they were unicorn covers or something. I don't know what that means, but I figured my sister would, so I grabbed her a copy."

"But," I begin as I show him two identical copies. "There are two."

He shrugs. "I built this amazing place down in Lexington and had them build custom bookcases in my office. I figure I need some amazing books to go on the shelves."

Once again, I'm stunned speechless.

"Maybe," he clears his throat again. "Maybe you could sign them for me."

I bite back the smile that is threatening to take over my face. He wasn't kidding when he said he likes me. Spencer Garrison likes *me*. Not Adeline Snow with the heels and the hair and the makeup. Just Agnes. With the weird name and the funny glasses and social awkwardness.

"I'd love to." And I really would. But as I fumble around in my bag I realize, "I don't have a Sharpie, though."

"That's okay." Spencer takes the books from my

hand and carefully places them back in his duffle, like they're precious and he doesn't want to ruin them. "I know where to find you."

The twinkle in his eye is back and the shyness is gone. I don't know how he can turn on the confidence so easily, but it's an inspiring sight to see. An idea for my surfer pops in my mind and I grab my notebook quickly, jotting down my thoughts.

It doesn't take long for the shuttle to come to a screeching halt and half the people standing stumble forward. Thank goodness I got to sit down this time. I would have been one of those people only there's no way I would still be standing.

Fortunately, we get to the gate right on time and zoom to the front of the line. It takes a second for me to understand why no one protests Spencer cutting in front of everyone, but then I see it. We're in first class. I gape at the sign for a second too long, making Spencer do a double take.

"What's wrong?"

I shake my head. "The entire time I've worked with my agent, I have never once been booked first class for anything. You really are my good luck charm."

His low chuckle reminds me I'm actually speaking my thoughts, not just thinking them. "What?"

"Nothing." I wave him away, hoping my face isn't flaming red but not holding much stock in that desire. "Nothing at all. Just glad we made it on time."

The gate agent calls us next and before I can think too hard about it, we're on the airplane, seated on the most comfortable cushions my butt has ever had the pleasure of using for air travel.

"This is amazing!" Spencer chuckles at my outburst, never opening his eyes as he leans back and absentmindedly rubs his knee, but this time I don't care if I made a social faux pas. Seriously. There are only twelve of us sharing a restroom? I never even knew that was something I cared about so much!

A smiling flight attendant approaches our little area and offers us a beverage.

"What do you want, Aggi?"

He called me Aggi. Butterflies take flight in my stomach, despite us still being on the ground, at him using my given name. It may not seem like a big deal to anyone else, but to me it's symbolic. Like he's choosing me over my carefully crafted persona. It's a big deal, even if I can't admit to it out loud yet.

"I think I'll have a white wine. You have that in first class, right? I've never been up here before."

Spencer chuckles again although our flight attendant seems slightly less amused. I wouldn't be surprised if she asked me to whip out my ticket right now to verify my seat assignment.

"We sure do. And what for you, sir?"

"Rum and Coke, please."

"Coming right up."

She saunters away, leaving me to enjoy the thrill of extra wide seats and leg room I don't need. You'd think I'd never been on a plane before with as thrilling as this is. But really. When did my people become such big spenders?

"I need to send them a thank you note," I murmur.

"What?"

Oops. Words came out of my mouth again.

"Nothing. Do you always fly like this?" I ask, criss-crossing my legs on the chair and flipping through the channels of the tiny personal television set in front of me.

"In first class?"

"Yeah."

"Most times. I need the leg room."

Looking down, I almost feel bad that some poor schmuck in the back needs this floor space more than I do. Almost. But then the flight attendant comes back and all is forgotten.

"Thank you!" I grin widely, knowing my excitement probably makes me look like I am fresh from the loony bin, but I don't care. "Ooh, this is so good," I say, downing my beverage from a real glass. Not a plastic one. Seriously, the rich and the famous know how to do things right. "Can I have another one?" She nods and magically appears with a second glass of white. "How's your rum and Coke?"

"Not quite as strong as I like it," Spencer says as we hear the doors close in the background, "but it's good."

"Wanna try my wine? I bet nothing on an airplane has ever tasted this fancy before."

He chuckles again, a sound I'm coming to love, and shakes his head. "No thank you. I'm good with my manly drink right here."

I pull back and give him a mock glare. "Manly drink? Are you calling my wine less than manly?"

"Aggi." There's my name again. Swoon. Maybe drinking on an empty stomach wasn't a good idea. "You and your drink couldn't get any less manly."

I gape at him. "I beg your pardon. We are very manly, thank you very much."

He smirks, which is suddenly my new favorite look on him. "Aggi, you're holding your pinkie up in the air when you drink."

"I am not!" And then I look down. "Oh. Huh. I guess I am."

He laughs again, and it makes me happy to see the smile on his face. I did that. Agnes Sylvester put a smile on the great Spencer Garrison's face. Now I understand why women talk about feeling powerful.

No, actually I've never heard a real woman say that before. I've only read it in romance novels. But still. Now I understand it.

"I think you need to slow down on the drinking. Our flight's not too long and I don't have enough arms to carry you and two suitcases through the airport."

Waving my hand dismissively, I take another sip. "Oh pish posh. I'll be fine. But seriously, you need to try this."

Reaching my glass over in offering, the plane takes

that exact moment to lurch, spilling most of my wine right on Spencer's lap.

Mortified and regaining my wits faster than I lost them in the first place, I place my glass on the tray and pick up my napkin. "Oh my gosh, Spencer. I'm so sorry! Let me help you."

Before I get to my target, Spencer's hand wraps around my wrist, stopping my motion. "Don't," he growls.

"Wha-what?"

With amusement in his eyes his gaze reaches mine. "I don't think you really want to turn this into a cliché romance scene, do you?"

"I—what?"

That smile is back. "Look what you were about to do."

Looking down slowly, realization hits me. I was about to wipe wine off Spencer's lap. Which means I was about to grab his junk.

Pulling my arm back like I'm being burned, I throw my hands over my mouth. "I don't want to be part of the mile-high club!"

The laugh that comes out of Spencer is so loud and so long, people begin staring. "Ohmygod, did you— did you just say you don't want to be—?" He's laughing so hard he's wiping tears from his eyes.

First class is suddenly not as fun as it was before the wine. Crossing my arms over my chest, I grumble, "At least I didn't make a joke about you talking in a gravelly voice and being hard."

That does it. The belly laughter starts all over again. Spencer laughs so hard the flight attendant comes over to see what the fuss is about.

"Is everything all right?"

"Yes. She—" Spencer gives up trying to explain and waves her away, but not before taking our empty glasses and reminding us to put our tray tables away.

"I'm glad you're enjoying yourself so much this morning," I snap as I settle in my seat. I can't help the irritation that floods through me. Although to be honest, part of me wants to laugh too. If I wasn't feeling humiliated, I probably would. And who knew wine in the morning let my claws come out?

"Aggi, if the rest of the trip is going to be like this, we're going to have one hell of a tour."

Spencer continues to chuckle long after I'm staring out the window, watching our plane hover above the clouds, leaving the East Coast behind.

Chapter 14

Spencer

Next stop: Minneapolis
Home of the Summer X Games, circa 2017 – 2020

I thought Philadelphia cold had a bite to it. Nope. I was wrong. Minneapolis doesn't just have a bite. It has giant monster teeth ready to chew you up and spit you back out. Holy balls, it's cold. Of course we are here during a week of "abnormally cool temps for this time of year" or some other bullshit statement every-one has said to us about the weather. Apparently, it's usually a little bit warmer here and, as luck would have it, will be about fifteen degrees warmer. Next week. Call me a baby but I'm a kid that grew up in Texas and now lives in California. I don't do winter.

Ambling over to the thermostat that doesn't seem to be doing jack shit to heat up my new hotel room, I listen to my sister prattle on in my ear.

"But is she nice? Not just fake nice but for real nice? No don't tell me. I don't want to know. But I kind of want to know."

I roll my eyes. This is why I've avoided her calls for the last couple of weeks. The second she found out I was going to be in close contact with her idol, I knew my cell company would start questioning my data plan and the fact that my minutes usage skyrocketed.

"Yes, Kate. She's very nice," I deadpan as I bang on the thermostat again. Why isn't anything happening?

"Don't patronize me, Spencer Garrison. This would be like me spending three weeks with Tony Hawk."

I snort a laugh because she's dreaming if she thinks her husband would ever let her near a superstar. He's no dummy. He knows he snagged himself a good woman in my sister and he would never risk her falling for someone else. No hall passes for that man.

"I'm not patronizing you. She's lovely."

"Lovely?"

"Yeah. She's funny and witty and so good with words. Well. Words on paper anyway." I smile when I think about how *not* good she is with words in person sometimes. "She makes me laugh and she's pretty good at photography. When she laughs, she does this weird thing—"

Kate gasps, stopping my tangent. "Oh. My. God. You *like* her!"

Shit. The last thing I need is for my sister to blast that on social media, so I go right into denial mode.

"Of course I like her, Kate. She's a likeable person."

"Oh no you don't. You *like* her like her, Spencer, and don't try denying it." She gasps again, and I know where this is headed. "Ohmygod, do you love her? She's going to be my sister-in-law, isn't she?"

"Slow your roll there, crazy pants."

I spend the next twenty minutes doing damage control with Kate. I'm not sure she's buying a single thing I'm saying, so finally, I cut her off. "Kate, I know this is exciting for you and I get it. Adi is pretty fantastic and you're right, I do like her. We're becoming friends. And, it's because she's my friend that I don't want anything negative to get out about us hanging out. You know how social media can be. She's sweet, and it wouldn't be fair if people made the wrong assumption and some of those crazy groupies started harassing her. This is her career, Kate. I don't want to screw that up. So, can we just agree that we're friends and having fun traveling together?"

The line is quiet. Too quiet, in fact, that I pull the phone from my ear to check the connection. Still there. Finally, I hear my sister speak.

"You're right. Sorry. You know how excited I get. I want you to find someone, Spence. And I haven't heard you speak of anyone like you were Adeline. Besides, if you were dating her and then married her and gave me nieces and nephews, I'd for sure get early copies of all her books. Oh! Even the foreign translations! I love those covers. Don't you think?"

"I'm so glad you have your priorities straight, sis," I say with a resigned shake of my head. "I gotta go. I'm meeting Adi soon. We have an event tonight and then another tomorrow morning before we head to Aspen."

"I'm still jealous you're going to Aspen for four days."

"Don't be. We'll probably sleep the entire time. I'm just glad I had the forethought to call Slade to use his condo. I'm over this hotel living."

"I can imagine. Call me next week, okay?"

Once I agree to call Kate next week and then accept a chorus of goodbyes from my nieces, I hang up the phone and plug it in before tapping my music icon. As the beats of Social Distortion's "Story of My Life" fill the room, I step into the bathroom for a shower and shave. The shower feels great as the water beats on my neck, especially since the water is hot and I can't seem to get the damn heater to work. I need to call the front desk about that.

Focusing on getting the spray on a particularly knotted up muscle in my back, I curse my ailments. I never thought making a career out of the sport I loved as a kid and excelled at as a teenager would lead to so many aches and pains. The constant kink in my neck from traveling and sleeping in beds that aren't mine is yet another reminder that retirement is something I need to get serious about. Ultimately, I'd like to have a family, be the dad who is coaching Little League, the retired skater who teaches both his son and daughter how to flip a board before they're old enough for kindergarten. If I don't start taking care of my body, those moments may not happen. I can't bend and lift like I used to.

Getting old is a bitch. A fickle bitch.

After showering, I stare at my suitcase and contemplate tonight's signing. The last few events, I've kept it pretty casual with my clothes but tonight I feel like stepping it up a bit. Aggi is always put together. Her Adeline Snow persona is obviously into fashion and has a special style about her. I should try not to look like a skater bum standing next to her. Instead of the Henley I planned to wear, I pull the ironing board and iron from the closet and set about smoothing out the wrinkles of my dress shirt. I'm not the best ironer but at least I won't look like I just rolled out of bed. Or maybe I will. It's cold as balls in here. If I don't get some clothes on soon I'm likely to get hypothermia.

I'm rolling the sleeves of my dark gray shirt up to the elbows when my phone signals a text message. Grabbing my phone from the charger, I tap the message.

Aggi: I took a nap and now I'm tired.

Me: I hate that. Coffee first?

Aggi: You read my mind. I'm almost ready. Meet you at the elevators in ten?

Me: See you then.

Slipping into my shoes, I sit down on the bed and realize for the first time that ten minutes is a really long time. Time ticks by at a snail's pace and I briefly contemplate walking down the hall to Aggi's room instead of waiting at the elevator. If she only needed ten minutes, she's probably close to ready so it shouldn't be a big deal. I grab my wallet and exit my room but as soon as the door latches behind me, I look up and find the girl herself walking toward me.

"Ten minutes is a really long time," she says.

Laughing, I shake my head and walk toward her. "I was thinking the same thing. You look beautiful."

A blush creeps up her neck to her cheeks, and it's adorable as fuck. She is beautiful. Her hair is piled high, similar to how it was when we first met in Chicago. Her makeup resembles that of an old-school pinup calendar but it's her outfit that really blows me away. Her black dress is tight through her chest, her very on display chest, down to her waist as it flares out to the knee. Tiny white buttons start at her cleavage and dot down to the narrowest part of her waist. She looks classic and modern all at once.

"Thanks. You, um, you clean up pretty nice yourself."

I feel a slight blush of my own which is ridiculous. I'm used to women throwing themselves at me, so a compliment isn't that big of a deal, but coming from Aggi it seems huge. I step toward her as she smiles shyly and turns toward the elevators. We only make it three steps before Aggi stumbles and mumbles something about "stupid flipping high heels." I smile and shake my head but say nothing as I place my hand to her lower back in an effort to not only guide her but hopefully catch her if she eats shit.

The line at the coffee shop in the hotel lobby is long but moving quickly so we take our place. Making small talk, I hear the whispers and see people pointing a little at Aggi. Adi. I need to use her pen name tonight. She wasn't kidding that it gets confusing. Ignoring the whispers, she's telling me about a hike she wants to take in Aspen when I notice a woman getting a little closer to us than anyone else. My guard is up, and I move my body a little so I'm shielding Aggi, er Adi. Shit. After placing our order and paying, we step aside and wait for our coffees when the woman I saw approaching steps around me in front of Adi.

"Oh.My.Gosh! You're Adeline Snow. Right here. In the coffee place."

Smiling, Adi reaches her hand out to the woman. Excitedly, the woman shakes her hand and then lets out a sound I can only compare to a dog's squeaky chew toy.

"This is so great. I mean, I'm going to the signing. I have like fourteen books for you to sign and I cannot wait for you to talk about your process. I'm an aspiring author myself."

"Fourteen? Wow, that's so great." Adi looks nervous and unsure, but plays it off well, not stumbling over her words at all. "Thank you so much for your support. I really appreciate it. Pardon my rudeness; this is Spencer Garrison. He'll also be at the event tonight."

"Oh, I know who he is. I have a few posters for you to sign too. But, Adeline I am so glad to have this one-on-one time. I have a bone to pick with you."

I thought sports fans had balls, but this lady is something else. She's not only in Adi's personal space, she's a little aggressive in her posture. Hands on her hips and head tilted, I step toward Adi again, my hand once again resting on her lower back. This time, it's a gesture of protectiveness and support and not one to keep her from falling on her face.

"A-a bone?" Adi asks, her confusion evident.

"Yes. Bobby deserved his own story. You set it up perfectly in the beginning of High Altitude. Then by chapter fourteen he was dead. You murdered Bobby!"

The woman's voice raises with each sentence and I can feel the tension radiate off Adi as it does. People around us begin to stare, the sounds of the espresso machine are non-existent as the woman continues shouting. She's quite passionate about Bobby and his love match.

"The meet cute was perfect and then nothing. You ruined it!"

Her last words are sharp and full of venom. I look to Adi and see her chest moving rapidly. Her eyes are wide, and her breathing is less breathing and more huffing. It's almost like she's doing some weird breathing exercise. Lamaze. That's what it's like. The one time I watched my sister practicing her Lamaze breathing was a lot like this. Shit, she's hyperventilating.

"I hope you're happy with what you've done. Bobby deserved better!" With that final declaration, the woman stomps away. The crowd around us stares for a few seconds at the strangest scene they've probably witnessed at a hotel lobby coffee stand. I quickly turn my attention to Adi and stand in front of her. My hands run up and down her biceps as her breathing picks up speed instead of slowing down. Shit.

"This is why I don't do tours," Adi mumbles next to me. "I told my publicist it was too much, but she doesn't listen to me."

Squatting to eye level, she looks at me, wide-eyed. Fear dances in her eyes as she rambles on about her luck running out, so I do the only thing I can think of.

I kiss her.

It's quick and not really my best work, but I kiss her. Quick and with need, my lips touch hers and I'm gone. Gone from thinking rational thoughts and how this is in public and there are probably fifty phones aimed at us taking pictures or video. I don't care. I have wanted to kiss this woman since the first day I laid my eyes on her. With one hand on her waist and the other on her neck, I tug her to me and I feel the moment she gives in to the kiss. Her body molds to mine and her arms grip my biceps. I lick her bottom lip but instead of opening for me, she gasps and pulls back. The moment frozen in time. My heart beats rapidly as the realization of this kiss hits me. It's sweet and tentative, passionate and hot. Everything you want in a kiss, everything I've read in her books come to life. Shit, I sound like my sister.

"What . . . what was that?" she asks, confusion, excitement and maybe a little fear in her eyes.

"A kiss."

"Why did you do that?"

"I don't know. I mean we were standing here and then that woman was screaming, and you were breathing weird. I thought you might pass out, so I just did what I thought would help."

"Kissing me? You thought that was the way to stop my weird breathing?"

"I mean, it's kind of like CPR, right? Mouth to mouth or—or something." We both know that's the lamest excuse I could come up with. I've never been trained in emergency techniques but even I know mouth-to-mouth resuscitation doesn't include tongue.

Looking down at the ground I scramble to think of an apology that is more for making a scene than for the kiss. I won't apologize for that. It was fucking fantastic.

A laugh bellows from her and when I look up she's smiling shyly with her hand on her mouth. Taking a step toward me, she whispers, "You kissed me."

"I did. I'm sorry."

"Don't . . . I mean. I don't know what I mean."

Just as I'm about to tell her what I'm sorry for, the barista calls our names and places our cups on the counter. Stepping up to the counter, we grab the coffees and turn to walk away when I stop her.

"Hey."

"Yeah?" she asks, taking a sip from her coffee.

"Who's Bobby?"

"I have no idea but apparently I really fucked up killing him."

At that, we both break out in full belly laughs as we walk toward the signing room.

Chapter 15

Aggi

Next Stop: Aspen
Home of the Winter X Games, circa 2002 – 2018

To my surprise, the "super fan" was not quite as angry as she led me to believe at first. When the signing finally started, and we noticed her standing in line, Spencer got really tense, really fast.

Not sure what that was about. He's fast enough to get away if she started getting handsy.

I tried hard to give her the benefit of the doubt. Turns out, I was right. She was lovely. Okay "lovely" might be a stretch. She was still brash and assertive, but after she apologized for her display in the coffee shop, we got to talking and it became clear that she has an intense love of storylines and character development.

And maybe she needs to get out just a teensy bit more. But I wasn't going to say that out loud. No reason to poke the bear. Or Bobby's mama bear as the case may be.

Still, it had me wondering about my reaction. It's not unusual for me to hyperventilate when I feel anxious. Hell, most of my falling incidents are probably related to me not realizing I'm holding my breath. Yeah. We'll go with that as an explanation.

But what about that moment provoked such intensity?

It's the thought I've had over the last twenty-four hours, and now that we've landed in Aspen and are at the condo of one of Spencer's friends, I've come up with a three-part answer.

One: I'm exhausted. As a natural introvert, peopling takes a lot out of me. It's the main reason I'm never seen at after parties or drinking in the lobby after an event.

Two: I'm even more exhausted because I don't feel like I can relax around Spencer. Despite how nice he is and how much I enjoy being around him, he's still my muse. My inspiration. My fantasy. That means my guard is continually up. Even when he's in the hotel room next door, I'm always nervous. What if I snore really loudly and he can hear me through the wall? What if my key accidentally opens the wrong hotel room door and magically end up in his room only to catch him watching elephant porn or something equally traumatic?

Even worse, what if a fire alarm goes off and we all have to race down the stairs in our footy pajamas and I slip and fall and tumble down four flights of stairs to the death of my pride and inevitable internet viral stardom? I'm sure I'll end up on the Murphy's Law website at some point. There's so much that could go wrong.

And three: My. Looming. Deadline.

One would think that being on the road with the man that makes all my fantasies swirl into my brain and onto paper like a wizard, this story would be a breeze to write, especially after he kissed me. Because *OHMYGOD SPENCER GARRISON KISSED ME!* But it's not. Sure, I'll get a few pages jotted down here and there, but mostly I'm so busy ensuring I'm not making a fool out of myself while trying to come up with scenarios that will require mouth-to-mouth again that my brain won't work.

Feeling discouraged and admittedly hiding from Spencer under the guise of "working," I pick up the phone to call the one person who might be able to get me out of myself long enough to get rolling. Making sure to mute the television while it rings, I avoid looking at the screen. For an X Games fan, I dropped the ball and dropped it hard. Not five miles away the winter games are in full swing, while I sit on a guest bed like the dumb ass who never realized she'd be in Aspen at the same time the winter athletes were competing. Instead of packing my puffy winter coat, I packed my petticoat for a little extra flair. Because flair is really going to keep me warm in winter.

Seriously, how much more can I sabotage myself?

"'Ello?" a deep British voice answers, some weird echo in the background, distracting me from self-depreciating thoughts.

Pulling the phone away, I look at the number. Did I misdial or something? I don't know anyone with a British accent.

Nope. That's it, all right.

"Todd?"

"Yes. 'Ello Gov'na."

I shake my head, utterly confused already and we've been talking for all of two seconds.

"Are you auditioning for a role in *My Fair Lady* or something?" Seriously. This is so weird. Although it is Todd I'm talking to, so maybe it's not all that strange.

"'M practisin my British accent for yer book."

Furrowing my brow, I mentally race through the list of characters in the story he's working on. "Uh, Todd?"

"Yes, Love."

"There isn't a British person in that story."

"Oh, I know. Figured I'd spice things up a bit. Make 'em li'l more excitin."

"Also, you don't sound British."

He gasps, and I can practically hear him throw his hand over his heart dramatically, eyes wide, and a look of horror on his face. So not only is he trying to be British, but now he's channeling Nathan Lane in *The Birdcage*? Yes, the 90s classic is one of our favorites but I'm so confused.

"'Ow could you say that? Fer yer information, the

lass at the grocery thought I was really from England."

"The cashier who only speaks in Instagram hashtags? I'm not sure she's a reliable source. Also, you just switched to a Scottish accent."

He huffs and gives up. "Fine. If you want to stick with boring American English, that's what I'll do."

I just roll my eyes at his comment. "Todd, there is not one person in the book who is from Europe. Why would they need an accent?"

"To spice things up?"

"Todd—"

"Oh come on, Aggi! I wanna really show my range. How about if someone is Canadian, eh? You know there are lots of Canadian snowboarders, eh?"

"None of them are on my fictional *American* snow-boarding team."

"They will be once I add some 'ehs' to the sentences."

"And then it won't Whispersync for all my audio lovers. Todd!" I yell over him as he continues to try on new voices.

"What!"

Suddenly, I hear the echo in the background again and I come to a very gross realization.

"Are you—Todd did you answer the phone while you're in the bathroom?"

His pause is the only answer I need. Screwing up my face I can't help but yell "Eeeeeew!!!!"

"What? The acoustics are great in here."

I shake my head and snuggle down onto the half dozen pillows I've surrounded myself with. This is why Todd and I are best friends. As odd as he is, he's always entertaining.

"Speaking of my new gig as your numero uno narrator, how's the new book coming?"

I groan my response, giving myself away.

"That good, huh?"

Huffing, I push my hair off my face and close the lid to my laptop, tossing it on the cloud of pillows next to me. Why pretend I'm going to actually get any writing done? "I just can't seem to get in the right mindset. Honestly, I don't think I'll be able to focus until this tour is over. It's impossible to write with Spe—so many people around."

Thankfully, he ignores the very obvious direction change, sniggering instead. "I love you, but you're so full of shit."

Gaping incredulously, I quip, "How rude!"

"I'm serious, Aggi," he says with a chuckle. "You're in, what, Slade McConough's ski condo?"

"Yeah."

"Slade McConough. One of the world's best freestyle skiers in the world. The guy we've cheered on for years."

"Yeah," I squeak.

"And you are in his home. He probably has medals and equipment and maybe even a master bedroom where snow bunnies have rubbed out—"

"Todd!" I yell.

"—his sore muscles, ya perv." Okay, he got me there. "Wander around with your Spotify list on from your last book. Check out his book shelves and toiletries. Sit on the balcony and watch the skiers go down the mountains. Go through his underwear drawer."

"I'm not going through his underwear drawer, *Todd.*"

I can practically hear him waving me off. "Missed opportunity. My point is, you are in Aspen, baby. There is inspiration all around you. Get out of your head and let it flow. You're going to some of the events, right?"

"No," I whisper, ashamed once again at my epic fail.

"Aggi! Are you kidding me? Why not?"

Throwing the covers off me I sit straight up. "I didn't cross reference the dates and didn't exactly pack my heavy coat for walking from the airport to the car, from the car to the building. It's actually winter here." I argue. "Besides, my schedule is usually pretty tight I didn't think we'd have the downtime. Also there have to be a million people. It's crazy here."

"Ugh, Ags. I love you, but you are losing it."

As much as I hate it, he's right about one thing. I have to get out of my head. My anxieties and insecurities about this whole tour are making it exponentially harder to focus. That's not Spencer's fault or my publicist's fault or the fans' s fault. It's my own doing.

"Maybe you're right."

"Of course, I'm right, love," he says in his horrific accent again.

"Still no to the cockney."

"Dammit," he mutters. "So, other than forgetting the biggest event of our lives down the street"—I roll my eyes as he continues—"tell me how the tour has been so far."

We chat a little longer about everything from the tour to his mom to my editor Greer's unexpected pregnancy. I had no problem shouting "I told you so!" when I got her text. Thoughts of writing a book about her pop into my head again. I jot it down on my list of storylines I'll probably never get to.

Eventually, though, we run out of topics and I realize I'm avoiding again.

Sighing, I give in. "I guess I should actually go crank out some words now."

"Yeah," he adds. "And I need to start voicing this book for real."

"Wait," I say as a thought comes to me. "You haven't started yet?"

A muffled sound comes through the phone, like he just shrugged with the phone too close to his shoulder. "What can I say? You're not the only one who's afraid of majorly screwing up for all the world to see."

I blink rapidly a few times. "But, Todd, your audition was amazing. You could seriously be one of the greats in this industry."

He chuckles, and I know the moment of vulnerability is gone. "Of course I could. But do I really want to put that kind of pressure on the other guys?"

Shaking my head, I don't bother pushing. Todd is really, really good at being rock steady. That little glimpse of insecurity is all I'm going to get. "Yes. Yes you do want to put the pressure on the other guys. So hop to it. No don't hop. You have my same lack of agility. Walk slowly and carefully to your new studio."

"Will do gov'na."

"No accents!" I yell into the phone, hearing his deep laugh before the phone goes dead.

Tossing it to the side I pick up my laptop, unmute the television still playing the games in the background, and hope for some sort of fog to take me over, making the words flow from my fingertips. A rookie snowboarder is making a run. I watch as he picks up speed before making his way up and over the lip, his body twists and turns, spinning like it's the most natural movement before landing and doing it again.

Yeah, this should give me all kinds of fodder to write about, so I keep focusing.

Still focusing.

Focusing some more.

Stiiiiiill waiting.

"Dammit, Todd," I grumble. Maybe he's right. Maybe wandering around will do me good. But before I can decide that, I hear a soft knock on the door.

"Come in."

Spencer's handsome face peeks between the door and the jamb. "Hey," he says with a smile. "I thought you might need a break."

Dropping my head to my chest I answer honestly. "A break would insinuate I've actually gotten anything accomplished."

I see the door open wider and watch him step through. "But you've been up here for a couple hours. I thought you were working today."

Closing my laptop and once again tossing it next to me, I decide to level with him. "I've been fighting with this story for weeks and I don't know how to fix it. Todd thinks I'm stuck in my head and maybe walking around the house will do me some good."

He looks confused, so I elaborate. "To get some inspiration."

"Why would walking around the house give you inspiration?"

Realizing Todd's suggestions would sound creepy to the wrong ears, I opt to play it off. "Oh ya know. Gets the blood flowing to my brain and all."

He nods and lets it go, thankfully. "Well, if you need inspiration, I actually know a great place to go to get it."

"You do?"

A wolfish grin crosses his face. "Yeah I do. I can't believe I didn't think of this before. How quickly can you be ready to go?"

"Go? Go where?"

"Nu-uh. I'm not telling you. It's a surprise." Now he has me intrigued, if not a little nervous. "Just dress for the weather and make sure you have your camera. I'll take care of everything else. But since there are reporters everywhere, make sure to dress like Adeline Snow."

Before I can even ask what he's talking about or why I should put my war paint on, he spins out of the room.

Spencer Garrison has a surprise for me. That's what we call a major plot twist.

Chapter 16

Spencer

Using my connections, or in this case ammo on a buddy, isn't my usual MO for a date. Okay, so reality is, I don't date much. But, tonight I'm counting this as a date. I knew when I saw the schedule that the Winter Games were going to cross with our event here in Aspen. I'm sure that's the entire reason we're here. When Aggi didn't say anything about it, I thought maybe she was only interested in the Summer Games as a spectator.

When she went upstairs to work earlier today, I did some laundry, checked in with Kate, and then went to town to scout a few possible locations for a Garrison Foundation park. The idea of seeing if she wanted to at least get out of the condo and grab some dinner was heavy on my mind all day but the moment I stuck my head in her room and saw the look of frustration and annoyance on her face, I knew I needed to step up that plan.

So, with a quick call to a friend, and a threat of posting his naked ass in a pair of chaps on social media later, I have two VIP passes to all the events for the next two days. Tonight, I thought I'd take Aggi to an exclusive club that not only has an open bar with amazing food, but the views of the various competitions is beyond anything we could see standing among the masses. Plus, we'll get to hear some kick-ass tunes tonight with some major headliners at a concert. This is date gold for two extreme sports fans.

What I hadn't expected when I told her to meet me downstairs and dress for the weather was for her to appear looking like a toddler spending her first day on the bunny slopes. With more layers than I could count, she looked ridiculous. And adorable. Her arms stuck out a little at her sides and the two scarves she had wrapped around her neck made it almost impossible for me to see the lips I've been thinking of non-stop since my attempt to calm her in Minneapolis.

I know Slade keeps a few extra jackets and pairs of snow pants around for when he has guests, so I went rummaging through the closets until I found a set I thought would fit Aggi after sending her off to change.

Finally, she's reappeared in a pair of tight fitted jeans and a snug white Henley with only one scarf around her neck. I stop walking and stare at her. Gone is the messy bun on her head that screams Aggi and in its place is a sleek side ponytail. Her glasses have been removed and while she's wearing makeup, it's still light and shows off her natural beauty. There's no denying it; Adeline Snow is a beautiful woman. But Agnes Sylvester is fucking perfection.

"You know I'm going to freeze to death the minute

I walk out of that door," she sasses, and I laugh.

"That's why I found these for you. Just slide your sweet ass into these pants and put on this jacket."

"Excuse me?" She gasps. Shit did I say that aloud? By the look on her face, I did.

"Sorry. I mean, here ya go, put on these pants and we'll be on our way to your surprise. Where's your camera?" I walk away, leaving her standing in place staring at me, her arm outstretched with the pants in her hand and her mouth wide open. It's probably best to run now before I get a tongue lashing. To my surprise, instead of a lashing as I walk from the room, she breaks out into a fit of sweet giggles.

"Sweet mother, it's cold out here. What level of crazy do you have to be to choose to live here?" Aggi has been going on about the freezing temps for the last fifteen minutes as the shuttle takes us to the mountain. Laughing as I pull her close to me, I sling my arm around her shoulder, rubbing my hand up and down her arm in an attempt to give her some warmth as the shuttle slows to a stop and the other riders begin stepping off the bus. When it's our turn, I grab her hand and tug her behind me.

The ride is not that long, but the warmth is welcome, downright exciting for Aggi. So much so that the moment we step from the bus, she gasps and mumbles about the cold again. Laughing, I step out of the crowd of people walking and pull her behind me. When we're far enough from the crowd, I turn to her and pull the beanie from my head and tug it onto hers. Eyes wide, she looks up at me confused and I grip her chin between my thumb and forefinger. The need to kiss her nags at me but I push it aside. Later. Right now, my girl needs to have some fun and get out of her head. My girl. Odd that's how I think of her now, but the idea of it makes me smile and not want to run for the hills.

"That'll help you stay warm."

"Bu . . . but you'll be cold."

"Nah, Aggi. I'll be just fine. You ready for the night of your life?" Smiling, she nods, and I hold out my hand to her. Hesitating only briefly, she looks from my extended hand to my eyes and back down before placing her small palm atop of mine and following me through the crowd to the area marked "VIP".

•••

When Slade told me about the VIP area and offered me passes, I blew him off telling him neither Aggi, or Adi as I referred to her, or I were interested in crowds or having to be "on" for any fans we encountered. He insisted the club area was chill and so full of celebrities and athletes that nobody would bother us. He was right. So far, nobody has noticed either of us, and we've sort of blended in with the crowd.

Well with the exception of Aggi stopping us when she ran into a Hemsworth and muttering a string of curse words and praises at the man. Thank goodness he's a skateboarding fan and was too busy fangirling over me to register her gushing about her love of Hannah Montana.

Other than that, it's been pretty tame here in the club.

I convinced her to take a shot with me to commemorate the occasion and now as I stand here holding our beers, I watch her as she snaps photos of the snowboarding event below. She's in her element, a small smirk permanently affixed to her lips. I feel the effects of the shot warming me and realize if I don't get some food in my system soon the liquor we're consuming will do more than warm me.

Nudging Aggi with my knee, I lean down and whisper in her ear, "Wanna get some food? I'm starving, and I saw a slider bar."

Aggi spins on her heel, eyes wide and dancing in the lights, with a huge grin on her face. "Spencer, this place is amazing. I cannot believe we're here. Todd is going to die a thousand deaths when I tell him. It's going to be amazing!"

Todd. I don't care what she says, no way that guy only wants to be friends with her. Aggi is too dynamic for him to never have noticed her appeal.

"Death. Sounds fine by me," I growl but she can't hear me over the cheers from below. Lifting her camera again, she snaps a few more shots before turning her attention back to me, taking the bottle of beer from my hand and lifting it to her lips.

"Did you mention food? I'm starving. Let's eat!" This time instead of leading Aggi through the crowd, she grabs my hand and tugs me toward the other side of the room where various stations are set up with food. We quickly make our way through the lines and fill our plates with various items from sliders to sushi to brownies before finding a small booth in the corner.

The booth is barely big enough for us to sit in and with my long legs, I have to sit close to Aggi, but she's so involved with her food she doesn't notice. I do though.

After we've eaten what is probably close to our own weight in food and thrown down a few more beers, we sit back in our seats a little and people watch a bit. You can tell the tickets for this club are expensive by the people walking around. There are more diamonds and furs in this space than I've ever seen in all my years living in California. Money drips from these people. Something I'm not used to.

"This is how I get some of my greatest plot points," Aggi says, breaking the silence.

"How's that?" I ask, taking a pull from my beer.

"People watching. It's fascinating. It helps to be the type of person that fades into the background. You can watch and observe without being noticed. You'd be surprised at some of the things I've seen and heard."

Interested, I signal to the cocktail waitress for two more beers and turn more to face Aggi, my arm resting on the back of the booth. "Yeah? Hit me with something."

"Well, there was one time I was sitting in the park watching people fly kites while I ate my lunch. I'd laid a blanket on the grass and was on my back, eyes closed, plotting out a book when someone sat on the bench nearby. At first, I ignored them but when I heard them say something about teddy bears, you could say my interest was piqued."

"Teddy bears?"

Nodding, she thanks the waitress and takes a long pull from her fresh beer before continuing. "Yeah. I didn't think much of it at first but then I realized it wasn't an actual teddy bear they were talking about. It was dressing up as a teddy bear. They were furries."

Confused, I have to ask. "Uh, what the hell is a furry?"

"In a nutshell, people who enjoy role-playing furry animals."

"No shit!"

"Nope," she says, popping the "p." "Sometimes they're fans of a particular television or video game character. Sometimes they create their own character to identify with. It's gaining speed as a fandom."

Shaking my head, I say "Okay that's random. What else ya got?"

She thinks for a second before giving me another. "I've watched men meet with their mistresses after hanging up the phones with their wives or women tearing tags off clothes and stuffing the new items in the bottom of their large bags. And, of course, there are the couples who obviously want to experiment and attempt to have sex in public."

"So you're a voyeur."

Her eyes widen. "What!? Ohmygod no! I don't *watch*, Spencer. I just see what I see."

"I'm kidding, relax. You ready to watch a little more of the boarding?"

Standing from the booth and taking her hand, this

time without offering, I lace our fingers together before walking to the edge of the viewing area. Putting her in front of me, I don't hesitate to step up behind her and place my hands on either side of hers, resting them on the railing. My body is close and I feel her stiffen a little. I lean down again and whisper in her ear, "Relax, Aggi. Watch."

Later when the concert starts, I'm still standing behind Aggi but now my hands are on her hips as she leans into my chest and sways her hips. She's not trying to be seductive or even sexual, but I can't help the way her movements affect me. We both stopped drinking a while ago and switched to water, so we can't blame our closeness on being buzzed or unaware. Flashbacks of dances in my teenage years come to mind and I laugh a little. That's what this is like. Being around Aggi reminds me of being fifteen-year-old me with a huge crush on the pretty girl. Unsure of what to do or how to behave, I can only rely on instinct, small touches and hand holding that I hope tell her I'm interested but don't scare her away. I have a feeling I need to take it slow and steady with Agnes Sylvester. It's going to be hard but the slow-burn between us will be so worth it.

Chapter 17

Aggi

Next Stop: Austin
Home of the Summer X Games, circa 2014 – 2016

A shift seemed to happen after our time at the Winter X Games and another successful signing. It's as if my entire body started to relax around Spencer. Not completely of course. There is probably never going to be a time I don't feel some sort of nerves around him or trip over my own feet.

But the intense anxiety, or maybe just his ability to "dazzle" me faded. Spencer stopped being my muse and started being himself. And as it turns out, the reality of him is better than any fantasy I could have dreamed up.

Spencer Garrison, the muse, is kind, athletic, hot and really good in bed.

Spencer Garrison, the man, is funny, chivalrous, protective. He's a good listener. He's an interesting talker. He's community oriented and an activist in his own way. Plus he's everything my muse is—kind, athletic, hot . . . and I assume he's still really good in bed.

I wouldn't know for sure, but let's face it. Even if he lasts as long as a sixteen-year-old boy on prom night, it would still seem amazing to me. Just holding my hand makes me break out in goosebumps up and down my arm.

I haven't stopped having goosebumps since that night at the games. Because Spencer, my handsome, rugged hero, loves to hold hands. In fact, he hasn't let go all day. He held my hand through the Denver airport, which is a very big airport. He held my hand when I fell asleep on him during our flight and ended up using his shoulder as a pillow.

Even the drool spot I left on his shirt didn't gross him out enough to unclasp his fingers from mine. It's all so . . . unexpected. Maybe even a realization that the version of him I had created is only slightly different than the reality. In my mind, Spencer Garrison was a lot of things, but a man who likes a little PDA wasn't one of them. I'm not complaining, just a little surprised is all.

Although, there haven't been any more kissing moments since his random, and out of this world, attempt to calm me in Minneapolis but it's as if we don't need them. We're taking our time with simple and small gestures and that works for me.

As we make our way through the airport, my hand in his, I envision to the outside world we look like one of those celebrities you see walking through LAX with the paparazzi taking pictures. Except we're at the Austin airport.

And there are no paps.

Or really any other similarity except that I'm holding hands with a hot guy. But that's not the point.

The point is, I feel like we're developing a real relationship and that both scares the ever-loving shit out of me and makes me more excited than I should be.

And yet, I'm a little sad we're about to pick up our luggage. Once we each have two bags, we won't have any hands free to stay connected. Total first-world problems, I know.

"So this is home, huh?" I ask as we wait for the baggage drop to begin.

"One of them."

"You have more than one home?"

He chuckles. "I just built a house here. I want to make a permanent move back eventually. It's been so long since I've called it home, I guess I'm technically still a Californian."

"Move back? You lived here before?"

This is news to me. I've followed Spencer for a long time, so I knew he was based in California, but never realized he had ties in Texas. My stalker abilities appear to have failed me.

"I was actually born here," he explains. "We lived in Lexington, where my house is now, until my parents got divorced. My mom and I moved but Dad was still in Lexington. Until I signed my first professional contract, I spent my summers here. There aren't really many places for training in the middle of nowhere Texas so visits sort of faded away."

I ignore the sadness in his voice at the loss of time with his dad, and instead concentrate on the part that is guaranteed to make him happy. "Weren't there places to train in Austin?"

"I'm sure I could have found somewhere. But with my dad working full time, it's quite a drive from our tiny town to get into the big city. You'll see."

"Wait. Are we going there tonight?"

"You didn't see the email?"

"What email?"

He laughs. It's that low rumbly sound that makes my stomach flutter but suddenly doesn't make me want to run and hide anymore. "You really need to get a smart phone, so you can keep up." I purse my lips at him making him laugh again. "San Francisco and Austin both got pushed back by a couple days, so we have some downtime."

"Oh." I try and fail to keep the disappointment off my face. "I guess I should fly home then."

A blush creeps from his neck up to his ears. "I, uh, I figured my house is close enough that we might as well get some use out of it."

My eyebrows shoot up. Holding hands is one thing. But we're going to Spencer Garrison's house?

His house.

Where his personal space is.

His bed. His bath towels. His underwear drawer . . .

Snap out of it, Aggi!

This shouldn't be a big deal. We've been sleeping in rooms next door to each other for two weeks now plus, we just shared a condo in Aspen. But suddenly my nerves are back full force. That was before. Before hand holding. Before lingering hugs and looks.

"Uh, that's okay, right?"

"Yeah! Yeah, it's fine," I say a little too quickly as I come back to my senses. "I mean, are you sure you want me there?"

"Yes," he almost yells, causing my head to snap back. "Sorry. What I mean to say is its really quiet and peaceful. It would be a great place for you to get some work done without outside distractions. Plus the guest bath has a huge garden tub to relax in. I know you're still kind of stressed about this deadline and a slower pace might do you some good. But only if you want to," he seemingly tacks on as an afterthought.

I nod my head a little too vigorously, my excitement mixing with nerves. "It's great. Thank you. And I guess this is how our publicists are able to spring for first class tickets, huh? Canceling a few days of hotel rooms?"

He gets a strange look on his face, but I dismiss it, mostly because I know myself well enough that because of my nerves I'm probably misinterpreting a lot right now.

"Oh! That's us!" Spencer jogs over to the carousel where magically both bags have dropped at the same time. Seriously. Does that man always rub good luck on me at the airport?

I try not to think about the loss of warmth from our hand holding as we drag our bags out the doors and through the parking garage. Actually, I don't have to try for long considering how quickly our bodies warm up once the humidity hits us.

"Ew. Isn't it still January here too?"

I could really get used to the sound of the chuckle that comes out of him. "Welcome to winter in Central Texas. It snows once every seven to ten years and might stick for an hour or two. But if you're lucky, you might be able to break out a thin jacket at least a couple of times before summer comes back again."

"You mean spring?"

"No, I mean summer. There is no other season here except summer. Unless Christmas counts as a season."

We climb in his black four-door pickup. I hadn't expected Spencer to drive such a huge monstrosity of a vehicle but somehow, it fits this part of him. The inside is plush and has all the bells and whistles I'd expect for someone of his wealth, but it's not much different than my rinky-dink car when you break it down. The large screen in the middle of the dashboard intimidates me just like the one in my little compact, only Spencer doesn't even look at it as he backs out of the parking space like I do. I need that little screen to help me maneuver in and out of tight spaces, and the little chime when I'm too close to an object is more than welcome in my car. He doesn't need it though. Instead, he turns slightly in his seat and whips his beast right out of the space like it's nothing. Show off. Pulling up to the kiosk, he pays the exorbitant parking fees and we hit the road. As we drive, I keep looking out my window, hoping to spot downtown Austin because I hear it's a beautiful sight, but I never find it.

"I thought Austin was going to look more like a city."

He furrows his eyes as he looks over at me, then jets his eyes straight back to the road. "What do you mean?"

"There's just a lot of open land. I wasn't expecting that."

"Oh. Well, we're going around Austin to get to Lexington."

"We are?" I try to keep the disappointment out of my voice, but I know there's still a tinge of it bleeding through.

"We'll see it when we come back for the signing. The airport is south of town so it's faster to not go through the actual city proper. Whoever created the upper/lower deck was an idiot. I don't how they thought it was going to help keep traffic moving."

"Upper/lower deck?"

"Never mind. I figure we can come in early the day of the signing and do some sight-seeing then."

"Can we go to the Capitol?" I ask. "I really want to work on some lighting and camera angles. The pictures I've seen of the building are beautiful."

Even thinking about the architecture makes me giddy.

"Capitol it is. I'll even show you the spot where no secrets can ever be kept."

"What?"

"You'll see." I swear there's a gleam in his eye, like it's another surprise he's keeping hidden until the exact right moment.

I relax in my seat as we drive, enjoying the hum of the engine and the quiet calm Spencer exudes. And, of course, those goosebumps come back when he reaches for my hand.

Just as I feel myself zone out and maybe even start to doze off a bit, a sign catches my eye. Sitting straight up, I point at it.

"Wait, that's Flinton?"

"Huh?" Spencer doesn't even bother to try and hide his confusion.

"We're in Flinton, Texas."

"We're driving *by* Flinton, Texas, but we're not in it."

"Oh my gosh. My editor lives in Flinton."

"Really? How random is that. That's only about thirty miles from where my house is."

"Wow. You guys are neighbors and didn't even know it." Realization makes my stomach plummet. "That also means I have to make a phone call. Do you mind?"

He shakes his head. "Not at all. Like I said, we've got about thirty miles to go."

Grabbing my phone out of my crossbody purse, I flip it open and dial, steeling myself for the tongue-lashing I'm about to get.

"If you hear me throw up just give me a second to finish."

My laugh comes out as a snort and I try to ignore Spencer's resulting grin. Instead I focus on my poor editor, who has just given me a gigantic dose of birth control.

"That's good, though, right? It means the baby is growing?"

"Growing. Thriving. Sucking the life out of me until there's nothing left except the hollow shell of a middle-aged woman. However you want to look at it."

I snigger. "My dear Greer. It appears you have taken over my role as the theatrical one in this relationship."

"A little role reversal has never hurt anyone. Do you have my chapters yet?"

I grimace. I should have expected that. Greer has always been sharp as a tack and focused. It appears pregnancy makes her more, well, we'll call it assertive as well.

"I've got, like, ten thousand words."

"Uh huh. And how much of that is random dialogue you've written down, so you don't forget it later?"

Busted.

Abort! Abort! Divert her attention!

"So you're pregnant, huh?"

That elicits a laugh from her and I know she's not angry, just worried about my deadline as much as I am.

Sighing, I level with her. "I'm still struggling. We went to the X Games and I took some good pictures and I thought it would help, but it still isn't coming."

I feel Spencer squeeze my hand in support, making the goosebumps come back.

"Adi." I brace myself, knowing that tone. "You are literally on tour with your muse. You can always ditch what you've got and write about this experience instead. Your fans would love it."

I try to control my breathing, and I'm praying Spencer didn't overhear what Greer just said. Judging by his over the shoulder look as he changes lanes, I think I'm okay. But what if he heard? I would be mortified. So much so, I'm not sure I'd ever recover—

"Adi, did you hear me?"

"Yes," I squeak out. Spencer gives me a strange look, but I don't respond and hope he doesn't figure out the noise is about him.

"He's sitting next to you, isn't he?"

"Yes." Another squeak. Another look. Another prayer of thanks that my phone accidentally fixed itself and I don't have to take calls on speaker anymore. Another mental note that maybe I should make the time to upgrade.

"Say no more. I'll keep my trap shut. Unless I'm throwing up."

That earns a giggle and a grateful sigh from me.

"I promise I'm still working on it, Greer. We have a couple days and are headed into small town Texas, so I'll try to focus. In fact, I just realized how close you live to Austin, so I hope you'll swing by the signing?"

"That's my plan, babe. Even if it's just to get a hug and meet this amazing man, I hope to come by. Just . . . have a garbage can right in my line of sight, would you?"

Aaaand another shot of birth control.

"I'll see what I can do."

"Speaking of. I gotta go. I'll . . . oh no—"

She doesn't disconnect before the sound of retching begins. Tamping down my own gag reflex, I hang up quickly.

"You look like you're about to upchuck."

Tossing my phone on the floor like touching it will get me sick too, I know he's not wrong. "Listening to your editor have morning sickness in the middle of the day will do that to you."

"She's pregnant?"

"Yep. First trimester. There's nothing that reminds you you're not ready to have kids as much as listening to someone else's misery as they grow a tiny human."

He cocks his head at me in question. "Does that mean you want kids someday?"

"Someday. But I need to get out of my second story apartment first."

He crinkles his brow. "You don't think it's safe for a baby to live with stairs?"

"No, I don't think it's safe for any baby if I have to carry it downstairs. Walking and chewing bubble gum are just about out of my realm of capabilities. Walking downstairs while holding a squirming, living being is a terrible idea."

Spencer laughs and squeezes my hand. I realize he laughs often. It's a great sound that brings a smile to my face. A short time later, he turns on the blinker, indicating our arrival in Lexington.

The road forks and instead of turning toward what I can tell is the downtown area of town, Spencer veers left and out toward the outskirts of town. Just a few minutes later, we stop at a large gate, and he leans out his open window to punch in a code on his keypad. The gate opens, we proceed down a long driveway, and stop in front of the most gorgeous house I've ever seen.

Taking my seatbelt off, I can't peel my eyes away from the high peaks, the brick work, and the lush lawn.

"Spencer, it's beautiful," I breath.

"Home sweet home," he answers with a grin. "Come on. I'll show you around."

I don't waste any time climbing out of his car, my nerves magically fading away.

Chapter 18

Spencer

Watching Aggi take in my house fills me with something I can't quite put a name on. I spent almost an entire year designing the house, and seeing it through her eyes reminds me of seeing Christmas morning through a child's. She's touching each piece of furniture and walking slowly from room to room. Her eyes are the size of saucers when she takes in my office and the floor-to-ceiling shelves I mentioned before.

"I can't wait to display my signed Adeline Snow novels on those," I say, stepping behind her as she runs her hand down the intricate woodwork. When I slide my hands around her waist and bend down to whisper in her ear, she visibly shivers, and I love knowing I have that effect on her. "You can't forget to sign them before we leave."

"Okay." Her response is a whisper as I place a quick kiss to her cheek before grabbing her hand and continuing our tour.

"Down this hall are two bedrooms and a full bath."

"What's this door?" She points to a closed door at the end of the hall.

"Basement. Well, workout room and storage. I had a home gym set up down there and the other half is just a big storage space."

The moment we turn into the great room, she gasps. This space is what took the longest to design. Looking at it now, it's hard to believe how much detail went into the design, but I knew what I wanted and wasn't willing to compromise. The room combines the kitchen, dining, and main living space into one. A large rock fireplace fills one wall completely while another is nothing but windows. Well, doors. Doors that open and slide into the wall making the outdoor space part of the inside. The kitchen has all the bells and whistles of a gourmet kitchen. Sad to say it'll never be used to its fullest potential unless I hire a chef.

"This table is amazing." Aggi drops my hand and rushes over to the dining table and chairs that weren't here when I left a few months ago.

"It is. A buddy of mine owns a custom furniture business and made most of the pieces here. This wasn't here when I was home last." Mimicking Aggi's movements, I run my hand along the top of the table and make a mental note to call Landon and thank him for these pieces. They're beyond anything I could have imagined.

"Wha . . . what . . . holy shit, Spencer!"

I turn my attention to Aggi and see she's found the focal point of the property. While the outdoor living space is pretty fantastic, and the view across the property is next to none, I know she's freaking out about the custom skate park I built.

"Pretty cool, huh?"

"Cool?" she questions, turning to face me. Her hands are flying as she motions to the backyard. "It's a skate park. In your *yard*. Todd is going to die. That's not me being dramatic either. He may fall over from a heart attack. When we were kids, we would make these little ramps in front of his house and pretend to be professional skaters. I thought that was the coolest thing ever. But, this. This is beyond words."

"Want to walk it?"

I take the wide eyes and extreme head bob as a yes and open the door before grabbing Aggi's hand and walking her across the patio. We meander past the fire pit and outdoor oven, and across a patch of grass, me taking the time to point out little design features here and there. Really, it's just an excuse to keep holding her hand.

Finally, we stand in front of the mini skate park. I'm proud of this little park. It's not much different than the smaller ones I design for the inner cities, but it gave me the chance to really see what could be done with a smaller space.

Without much area to work with inside most city limits, I've come up with a few options that allow us to drop a skate park right in the middle of city block without much issue. And the design doesn't only cater to skateboards. Motocross and even scooters are welcome as well.

Sure, not everyone is respectful, or appreciative, of the efforts, but I'd rather have kids being active and perfecting skills than getting into trouble or locking themselves away in front of a screen.

"It's amazing, Spencer. I can't get over it." The sun is setting in the distance and its warm glow casts a soft light on her; I'm rendered speechless. Without a second thought, I rest my hand on her shoulder and spin her to face me before swooping down to capture her lips with mine.

Her response is tentative at first but the moment I wrap my hands around her waist and tug her close to me, she relaxes and her arms rest on my shoulders. The kiss is soft and slow, my tongue barely slips out but it's all the request she needs because my girl opens for me and it's lightning and thunder combined. A storm brews in me as I deepen the kiss, and I know there will never be another woman in my life who stirs this kind of response from me.

A soft moan escapes her and it's my cue to pull back. Slowing the kiss, I move my hands from her waist to her face, cupping the sides as I peck her lips once, then twice before resting my forehead on hers. Our breaths are labored, and a smile appears on both our faces simultaneously.

"That was . . ." she begins.

"Yeah it was." Sighing, I take a small step back, my hands still holding her face as my thumbs brush her pinkened cheeks. "How about we clean up before we make some dinner?"

"Oh . . . okay."

"Hey," I say. "We aren't done here. Not by a long shot. But, I want to take my time with you and out here on the halfpipe isn't where I want you for the first time."

A quick intake of breath from Aggi followed by a larger than life smile tells me she's just fine with that plan. She turns on her heel to walk away, and feeling playful, I smack her ass as I pass her in a light jog up to the house.

Thanks to my longer strides and the run, I reach the house first. I sent a text to Landon earlier today asking if he'd do me a solid and put a few groceries in the fridge for us, but I have no idea what he bought, so I immediately rush to the kitchen to assess the provisions. By the looks of things, Landon is making up for me not pressing trespassing charges against his girlfriend's kid.

The fridge is stocked with not only a few steaks and a small salad, but some breakfast foods, cold cuts, and bread. I'm sure if I check the pantry there will be chips and other basic snacks too. This is my favorite part of small town living. Knowing I have friends I can count on to help me out makes these impromptu visits possible.

"That's not fair," Aggi says between breaths. Closing the refrigerator door, I turn around to find her bent over, hands on her knees, gasping for breath.

"Sweetheart," I begin as I walk up to her, "did you run?"

Nodding, she gasps a few more times before standing up straight. "I . . . I . . . good lord, you're fast. I didn't want you to leave me standing here not knowing how to get back to the bathroom. This place is like a mini mansion, a girl could get lost."

"First, I wouldn't leave you anywhere. Second, it's not that big. Five bedrooms, four and a half baths."

"Five? I only saw two."

"Oh yeah, well two bedrooms on that side"—I motion toward the hallway we were down earlier—"plus the master down that hall and two more upstairs with the rec room."

"My goodness, do you plan on holding conventions here or something? Why do you need all that space?"

Shrugging, I run my hand through my hair and look down while I process my response. How do you tell the woman you're interested in and barely know that you built this house with a family in mind? That your dream is to fill this house with a wife and children to make it a home? "I like to have options. No big deal." I clap my hands to break the tension. "Now, let's get your bag, and I'll show you to the master bathroom. It's really the best part of the house. Have you ever used a shower with a rainfall showerhead?"

Shaking her head, Aggi follows me to where our bags are set and then down the hall to the master. The room isn't too fancy, but the bathroom is grand. Natural stone and distressed wood, it's like stepping into a cave. I designed this room for my future wife. A sanctuary for the woman I will spend my life with and who, God willing, will give me a family.

•••

"That was amazing. You were right; you are pretty kickass with a grill."

"Agnes Sylvester, did you doubt me?" I tease as we finish loading the dishes into the dishwasher.

Wiping her hands with the dishtowel, she shrugs before tossing the towel my direction and picking up her wine glass. With a chuckle, I twist the towel and playfully snap at her ass as she turns away from me. She yelps and inevitably spills some wine, thank goodness it's white, making me laugh some more, and I realize I've never had a more relaxed evening.

"Want me to top off that glass and start a fire?"

"Spencer, it's at least seventy degrees outside. Why would we have a fire?"

"It's romantic?"

"Is that a question or a statement?" She teases, the wine having relaxed her a bit.

After I showed Aggi the shower earlier, I left her to freshen up while I marinated the steaks. When she walked out of my room dressed in a pair of shorts and a black tank top with no makeup and her hair loose down her back, I almost fell over. The attraction between us has been building and in that moment, I wanted nothing more than to throw her over my shoulder and take her to my bed.

Instead, I told her to make herself comfortable and retreated to the shower. When I walked in my bathroom, I was assaulted by the overwhelming scent of vanilla, like I was walking into a field of vanilla beans. I'm not too proud to admit I almost had to take care of myself in the shower when I envisioned Aggi in it only minutes before. Naked.

I'm pulled from my lustful thoughts when she says my name again and reaches her hand out to my arm. "Are you okay?"

"Yeah, sorry. So no fire?"

"I'm okay without it. How about we just chill on the couch?"

Nodding, I grab the bottle of wine and follow her to the large sectional. I allow her to sit first, unsure if we're on the same page. We've been flirting, and I've managed to sneak in a few quick pecks to her lips since our kiss earlier but that's it. Aggi isn't overtly flirtatious like the women I've been around the last few years. She isn't thrusting her chest out or twirling her hair. Instead, she tosses out snark and tells awful jokes.

"Are you going to stand there holding that bottle or come sit your ass down and fill my glass?"

"Dang woman, you're a little demanding with wine in you."

Her eyes widen, and her mouth forms an "o" in response.

With a wink I say, "I like it. It's sexy when you're all demanding."

Blowing a raspberry, she rolls her eyes and takes a long sip of her wine before thrusting her hand my direction as I sit beside her.

"What was that response for?"

"I have never been sexy in my life."

"Aggi, you've been hanging out with the wrong men because you, sweetheart, are absolutely sexy. One of the sexiest women I've been around."

Seconds tick as I watch what I've said process in her mind. Tilting her head, she slowly takes a sip of wine like she needs the liquid to help her understand what I'm saying. Squinting her eyes, she pulls the glass from her lips and my gaze falls to where her tongue darts out to lick a lingering drop of wine.

Slowly, I take the wine glass from her hand and place it on the table along with my own before shifting my body and leaning forward. My hand glides up her thigh and to her waist, gently tugging her forward. Meeting me halfway I let her take the lead. When her tiny hand rests on my leg, my dick jumps in anticipation. Her lips are soft and her kiss tentative. Her hand grips my shorts as she deepens the kiss. That's all the resolve I have because in seconds, I grip her waist and tug her to my lap, her legs straddling me.

In the background, I hear the sound of her wine glass toppling over like she accidentally kicked it, but I dismiss it. I don't care about clean up, that can wait.

Arms draped around my neck, Aggi leans into me. Chest to chest, we kiss, we lick, we nip. My hands slide under her tank top and graze her skin lightly. I feel the goosebumps scatter her skin as I run my fingers up her sides, and when I reach her breasts, she moans and grinds her hips down my cock. I let out my own groan, or more of a growl, when I realize she isn't wearing a bra. Fuck. My. Life.

Unable to control myself, I lift my thumbs, so they

gently rub over her hard nipples. Aggi pulls back from the kiss, her head thrown back as she whimpers and mewls.

"Goddammit baby, you feel so good," I mumble between kisses to her exposed neck. Grinding, my girl says nothing in response but the way she's moving her hips tells me she wants this as much as I do.

Pulling one hand from under her tank, I reach for the top of the neckline and tug it down a little, exposing her nipple before lowering my head to take it into my mouth. Rolling my tongue around it, teasing before sucking, I listen to the sounds of a woman full of lust and need, and I know this night will change everything for us. There's no going back to simple flirting and holding hands.

Letting the nipple pop from my mouth, I tug her mouth back to mine as I stand, forcing her to wrap her legs around my waist as I walk us to my bedroom.

"Oh," we both say simultaneously as we bang our foreheads together.

Rubbing the red mark, she looks at me sheepishly. "Sorry. I guess my clumsy doesn't go away when I get horny."

All I can do is grin and keep walking. "I don't mind. I kind of enjoy that we can stop in the middle and laugh sometimes. Makes it more fun that way."

She blushes as I cross the threshold, kick the door closed, then pull back and look her in the eye.

"But on a serious note, I need to make sure you're sure. Are you? Sure?"

She nods, but I shake my head in response.

"Baby, I need you to say it. I need to know you're in this with me, Aggi."

"Yes, Spencer. I'm with you."

Those words are music to my ears as I lay Aggi down on my bed with every intention of showing her how sexy and irresistible she is. As I make love to her I don't want her to doubt how much she's come to mean to me, so I do my best to show her.

Chapter 19

Aggi

Slowly coming to my senses, I stretch my arms over my head and my legs toward the foot of the bed. This is probably the most comfortable mattress I've ever slept on. I should ask the hotel what kind it is, so I can get one for my bedroom. Sleepy time comfort is always a good investment.

Peeling my eyes open, I realize I'm not in a hotel room.

Suddenly, memories of the night flash through my mind:

Spencer kissing me.

Spencer pulling my clothes off.

Spencer taking his own clothes off.

Spencer using his tongue to—

Shooting straight up in the sitting position, I hold the sheet over my chest as I try to make heads or tails of my thoughts.

Maybe I dreamt it all. That's got to be it. I was

thinking about the book and ideas came to me in my sleep and it turned into an erotic dream. That's all it is. Right? It has to be. There's no way.

Right?

Deep breaths, Aggi. There's only one way to tell if that dream really happened.

Pulling the sheet back, I look down and see I'm naked as a jaybird.

Nope. Definitely didn't dream that. I had sex with Spencer Garrison. Amazing, passionate, heartfelt, and I'd do it again in a second, but it was definitely sex.

"OHMYGOD I HAD SEX WITH SPENCER GARRISON!" I shout to no one in particular, since I seem to be alone. Or at least I hope I am. My outburst will be very, very embarrassing if someone heard it. Plus, if no one is here I can claim that whole "If a tree falls and no one is there to hear it, it doesn't make a sound theory." That means it never really happened, right? *Right.*

Okay it made more sense before I thought too deeply. But nothing makes sense right now. Especially not how this all happened.

Pulling myself together, I find enough bravery to look for any signs of life outside of this really amazing bed. What are these sheets made of? Fairy eyelashes? "Um . . . hello?"

I listen.

And listen.

And listen some more.

Nope. No response.

"Is anyone home?" I try again as I rise from the bed and tug the sheet of the bed, wrapping myself like a little naked burrito. Well, a naked burrito wouldn't have a tortilla . . . nevermind.

Slowly, I open the door and stick my head into the hallway, shifting my eyes back and forth. I finally come to the conclusion that no one is here. Or at least in this side of the house. This place has enough square footage I'm sure anyone in the west wing wouldn't hear if I took a sledge hammer to the wall.

Of course the West Wing is actually in Washington D.C. and there isn't a sledgehammer in here anyway—

What am I even thinking about?!?

Refocusing on the situation at hand, I allow relief to flood through me that my freak-out remained private. Somewhat private anyway. I hear a strange scratching sound outside. Does Spencer have a pet I don't know about?

Before I can investigate, I have to find something to wear. We may have taken things to a new level last night—

Ohmygod I had sex with Spencer Garrison.

—but that doesn't mean I feel comfortable walking around this joint naked. This of course, leads to another problem.

I have no idea where my clothes are.

Scrunching my nose, I finally make the decision to grab a T-shirt from his dresser drawer. I don't think he'll mind, but I'm right smack in the middle of the "morning after" and my new lover has disappeared. At this point things could go a multitude of ways.

One: He thinks I look nice in his clothes and asks me to marry him and have all his babies.

Two: He thinks I look terrible in his clothes and demands that I leave immediately and never bother him again.

Three: He doesn't bat an eye either way, we have a nice breakfast and continue on with the tour, content in the knowledge that we had a wonderful night of mutual and consensual pleasure to draw memories from in the long and lonely nights of the future.

Honestly, any of those scenarios are both absurd and realistic.

Forgoing the pants because nothing Spencer owns seems to have drawstrings and pants are pointless if you have to keep pulling them back up, I slowly head out of the bedroom into the main living area. From here, the scratching sound gets louder and I can finally pinpoint what it is—Spencer is on his skateboard.

Excited at the opportunity to put my camera to good use, I find it in my bag and quickly make my way to the back where a very sweet setup awaits outside.

Sliding the door open, I step onto the patio. Holy balls it's cold.

Shivering, I regret not looking for another pair of pants. Or at least socks. I don't know where the humidity from yesterday went, but it's certainly not here right now.

Trying my best to remain unnoticed and not shiver in case he wants to run his hands up my legs later—

Ohmygod I had sex with Spencer Garrison.

—I watch through the lens as Spencer picks up speed, launching himself into the air and down a railing, sliding quickly to the bottom before pushing off again. Around and around he goes, from the bowls to the stairs to the railings and back, never slowing down. Always in motion. Always keeping in total and complete control of his board. It's mesmerizing.

Spencer gains more speed, and I watch as he dives back down into the bowl, popping out on the side closest to me and stops.

"Hi."

"Oh!" I lower the camera from my eye and throw my hand over my heart. "I should have read the warning label. You scared me."

"Warning label?"

"You know, objects in the lens may appear closer than they appear? Never mind," I say waving him off. "That was an amazing switch stance, by the way."

He raises an eyebrow in surprise. "So you *do* know your skateboarding."

I make a weird "pffft" sound with my lips. "What, did you think I was just a pretend fan? Would you like me to define the term for you?" Clearing my throat I begin reciting the definition in my most boring monotone voice. "To increase the difficulty, variety, and aesthetic value of tricks, riders can—" Before I'm able to continue, he steps up to me and places a finger to my lips. Damn I wish those were his lips and not his finger. I mean, it's a great finger and all but . . .

"You win. You're the real deal, babe. How'd you sleep?"

When he finally reaches me, he leans in to give me a sweet kiss, and it's then that I notice the sheen of sweat on his shirtless physique. A physique I've been up close and personal with.

Ohmygod I had sex with Spencer Garrison!

I don't necessarily feel it's appropriate to remind him I've seen him naked, so I fall back on the second-best part of the night.

"You have the most comfortable mattress in the world."

He chuckles against my lips and shrugs. "What can I say? I like my sleep."

Shifting back and forth on my feet, I bite my lip, not quite certain if I should ask what I'm thinking. Of course that means Spencer picks up on it right away.

"What's going on in that mind of yours, Aggi?"

Pursing my lips, I gaze out into the distance, uncomfortable with my question but knowing it'll be worse if I don't know. "Why'd you sneak out? Or did you sneak out? I mean, maybe it wasn't a sneak. Maybe it was a statement? Which its totally okay if it was. I know people have consensual sex all the time with no strings attached but I just want to make sure I'm clear on what's happening—"

"Aggi," he interrupts me. When my mouth closes

and I look back at him he continues. "I figured you would be a little freaked out this morning and wanted to give you some space to collect your thoughts. I knew you'd come find me when you were ready."

Oh.

"Oh."

"So have you collected them yet?"

Brushing a stray hair off my face I think about how to answer his question. Honestly, I'm not sure what I'm thinking, but I know most of it is based on how he would answer. So deflection. Deflection is my answer.

"I'd rather know if you were sorting through your own brain out here." I gesture with my head to his homemade skate park.

He shakes his head, amusement written all over his face. "Agnes Sylvester. Are you always so quick to try and divert my attention?"

Taking a deep breath, I make the impulse decision to lay it on the line. "Can you blame a girl like me?"

He reels back, crinkling his brow. "What does that mean?"

"Spencer, it's okay. I had a wonderful night with you. But you're, well you're you. Handsome and charming and"—my gaze drops to his oh so beautiful chest again—"really, really hot." I ignore his soft laughter as I continue. "And I'm just me. Clumsy and socially awkward and basically ill-prepared for life."

"Wait." He holds his hand up and takes a step back. "Are you insinuating that *I'm* somehow out of *your* league?"

The look on my face says "duh" but the words that come out sound more like, "You *are* out of my league."

"I'm not sure I like the way you think about yourself."

"It's not self-depreciating, Spencer. I'm just realistic."

Stepping forward again, he grabs my hand and brings it to his lips, kissing my knuckles and basically making me swoon all over again.

"Let me give you some more realism. Aggi, you are funny and smart. You are talented and creative. The way you spin basic words into engaging stories baffles me in the best of ways. I never know what's going to come out of your mouth, whether it be a joke or drool—"

"Hey!"

"—and I love that about you. You keep me on my toes, but you also keep me grounded. You understand why I love my job, but you also understand I don't want it to be forever because this is just a sport. The important thing is that people can be reached because of a platform I found in my childhood hobby. You get that. Not every woman does. So no. No you aren't out of my league. In fact, I'm almost positive we're in the same league. Maybe even playing for the same team. Batting for the other team."

A laugh bursts out of me as he realizes what he just said.

"Wait. Did I just accidentally come out of the closet?"

I nod, still laughing so hard I snort. "After last night, I can tell you I am just as surprised as you are. You were so far back in that closet I had no idea this would ever happen."

Grabbing me, he pulls me to him, hugging me. "I would try to correct my mistake, but I haven't had breakfast yet, so I'm pretty sure all I'll end up doing is digging a bigger hole."

He rubs my back, warming me up a bit.

"Besides, you're freezing."

"You noticed?"

"Ags, you have goosebumps all down your legs."

I groan and drop my chin to my chest. "Dammit. I didn't want to have to shave today."

He huffs a laugh and climbs over the low wall, intertwining our fingers. "Come on. Let's get you inside. You need heat and I need to eat. Come to think of it, we could probably take care of both those things in the bedroom."

His brash comment apparently throws off my equilibrium as I immediately trip over—actually, who knows? It was probably a piece of dirt or something. But Spencer, ever the hero, steadies me before I get close to hitting the ground.

"Maybe later. I think I need some coffee before my brain shuts off completely."

He grins, and we continue on our way.

A girl could get used to waking up like this.

Chapter 20

Spencer

When I woke up yesterday morning and knew I'd be taking Aggi to my home, I had no idea where we'd end up. Of course, I've hoped for the last few weeks we'd end up in bed together, but I also know Aggi well enough to understand that may not have happened. To my surprise, a few glasses of wine, a delicious meal, and good conversation is all it took for my girl to relax and be herself. The self I knew was there and the one I'm falling for.

Fallen? No, falling. It's too soon for more, but I know without a shadow of a doubt I have strong feelings for Aggi, and I only hope she stays out of her head long enough to develop some for me.

This morning, when I opened my eyes with the warmth of Aggi next to me, a feeling of peace flooded through me. Curled on her side with her hands nestled under her cheek, her bare back was peeking out of the sheet facing me. I wanted to wake her with kisses along her spine. I didn't. Instead, I threw on some clothes and snuck out of the room to let her sleep and wake up to process what I'm sure was an epic freak-out.

Deep down I knew she'd question us being together, not just the sex but the intimacy we shared. The way our bodies molded together, the way she lit up from the inside with each of my touches and the sound of my name on her lips as she came apart in my arms. I know Aggi doesn't let most people see her, she doesn't open herself up and show the world who she is. Trusting me with that part of her makes me believe we might be on the same page.

After our quick chat and my reassurance that we were okay, we walked inside and together made a huge breakfast. Then we showered. Together. Nerves prickled at Aggi in the light of day but the moment I dropped to my knees in my cave-like shower, she turned from nervous to empowered. Gripping my hair and begging for more as I worshiped her, she let go and it was perfection.

Now, with our hands linked as I drive into Austin to check in to the hotel before the signing, she's humming along to the soft music wafting through the cab. Comfortable silence. Comfortable together. That's us. Spencer and Aggi, just being together as we drive to one of the best cities in the country.

As we pull up to the hotel, I pull up to the valet and turn off the ignition. Looking to my right, I note my girl nibbling on her thumbnail. She's in her head. Again. I swear she gets herself spinning when she spends time alone with her thoughts, immediately going to the negative. I see the anxiety waft from her. Instead of saying something, I jump out of the truck and run around to her door, flinging it open. Jumping, she turns her head to me.

"Boo."

"Jesus, you scared me."

"Got you out of your head. Come on, sweetheart. We need to get checked in and then hit the Capitol building."

Smiling, Aggi places her hand in mine and hops from the truck. We both walk to the back of the truck and pull our bags from the bed before heading inside. Once at the front desk, I give the clerk our names and she taps the keys quickly before looking up to us and saying, "Mr. Garrison I have you in room ten forty and Ms. Snow, you're all set in room nine sixteen."

"Excuse me, but we don't need two—" I begin but Aggi places her hand on my arm, stopping me from continuing.

"Missy, would it be possible for us to have rooms next to one another or at least on the same floor? We're traveling together so it just makes things easier." I look at Aggi who isn't acknowledging me or the confused look on my face. I nudge her leg with my hand, but she only swats it away with a smirk on her face.

"Oh, let me see what I can do here." Tap tap tap. Missy's nails click-clack on the keys, her eyes focused on the screen. After a few minutes she looks up and nods. "I have two rooms in another tower, you'll be in five sixty-nine and five seventy-one. Will that work for you?"

"That's perfect. Thank you."

Taking the offered key cards from the clerk, we grab our bags and head for the elevator. Stopping in front of my room, I pause and look at Aggi.

"Sweetheart, you're not going in that room. We're staying together."

"I'm putting my things in here, Spencer." I watch as Aggi opens her door and pulls her bag in behind her. Then stumbles, the bag falls over, and she apologizes to the door as she falls on it.

"Can we pretend that didn't happen?"

"Of course."

The moment my door closes behind me, I let out a groan of frustration. I wanted to share a room with Aggi not keep having separate rooms. Things changed for us last night and again this morning. She knows it, and I know it. I want her with me. If she's alone, she'll only let her thoughts wander and spin out of control.

Knock. Knock. Knock.

Quickly, I turn my head to the noise and see the door adjoining our rooms. Unlocking it, I open my side and standing before me is my favorite girl.

"I didn't want to ask for adjoining rooms, but I hoped. We have to keep up appearances. And"—she crinkles her nose like she's gathering courage to share another part of herself—"I need my space, Spencer. I know you don't understand it, but this is hard for me. New. Different. I've never been this girl and I . . . I don't know what to do. I'm going to freak out and when I do, I'd rather you not witness it. It won't be pretty."

Grabbing her hand, I tug Aggi into my room and

spin her into my arms before lifting her and tossing her onto my king-sized bed. Lowering myself so I'm hovering over her, I smile as a string of giggles escapes her. Soft breaths skirt my skin as she blows hair from her face.

"You're not only the sexiest woman I know, Agnes Sylvester, you're the smartest. Appearances will be kept for now. As for the freak-out you expect to happen? How about you just let yourself enjoy this?" Lowering my mouth to her neck, I place a slow kiss to her skin while my hand runs up her leg. She sighs and relaxes into the mattress as I continue to place kisses along her neck.

"Okay." Her response is a whisper and I know she wants more. Wants my mouth on her body, my dick inside of her. But, I promised her a day at the Capitol, and I am a man of my word.

Jumping from the bed, I smack my hands together as she leans up on her elbows. Her cheeks are flushed, and her breasts rise and fall quickly along with her breaths. "Ready to hit the Capitol?"

"Now?"

"Yep. I promised you the Capitol and to show you the spot where no secrets are possible."

With a groan and what can only be considered a look to kill, Aggi rises from the bed, brushes her hair from her face, and walks into her room, grabbing her camera and purse from the bed before walking out the door to the hallway.

Appearances. Got it.

•••

"This place is amazing. Beyond what I thought it would be." The awe in her voice evident, I watch as Aggi clicks photo after photo of the building.

We started the walking tour with a group but have fallen behind a little, with me offering my own commentary. When I was a kid, my dad never knew what to do with me after the third week of my summer arrival. One year, he registered me for a day camp and one of the field trips was to the Capitol. At first, I thought it would be boring like school. I was wrong. Of course, it was educational and boring from time to time, but the grandeur of the building and grounds stuck with me and I would ask my dad to bring me here even when there was no camp.

"It is pretty awesome. But it should be. It's caught on fire enough times that they keep having to renovate," I chuckle as I watch her squat down and adjust her lens before rapid firing again.

She pulls away from her camera to look up at me. "Seriously?"

"Oh yeah. This isn't even the original building. It's the third one, I think. And we're lucky to be standing here since there was some sort of electrical fire in the 80s."

She shakes her head and goes back to her task; she is talking about the impressive lines and arches.

"I had no idea this building was taller than the Capitol in D.C. I'm sure some politicians were unhappy when that happened."

"You know what they say: Everything's bigger in Texas. I suppose it seems fitting that the egos are as well."

Draping her camera around her neck, she walks toward me, so we can continue our exploration. "You're a bit of a political nerd, aren't you?"

"Political? No. I probably hate politics more than social media, which is saying a lot. No, I'm more of a history nerd. And architecture interested me when I was a kid. I never expected skateboarding to be my career. I thought I'd pursue architecture as a career."

"That makes sense. This place is amazing, Spencer. Thank you for bringing me. The photos online don't do it a bit of justice."

"I agree. But there's more. I wanna show you something cool."

Taking Aggi's hand, I walk her to the famous star. The spot under the dome where whispers can be heard in the outer passages.

"Stand here." Standing toe to toe, I take the camera from around Aggi's neck and place it gently on the ground next to us before taking her hands in mine and leaning into her ear.

"They say, if you whisper something at this spot, even the people in the outer passages can hear you. There are no secrets in this spot. Anything said can be heard by all."

A quick intake of breath as my whisper tickles her ear makes me smile.

"Agnes Sylvester, I think you are the most beautiful and talented woman I've ever met. You have a kind heart and infectious laugh. I'm honored you're willing to spend time with me, and I promise I will never let you regret it."

Placing a chaste kiss to her cheek, I lean back and see she's closed her eyes and a small smile graces her lips.

"Thank you," she whispers before I lean down and kiss her, all while other visitors watch us, knowing an important declaration was just made.

Chapter 21

Aggi

Next Stop: San Francisco

Home of the Summer X Games, circa 1999 and 2000

I have never had a boyfriend before.

Not from lack of desire, but because I haven't met anyone who tickles my fancy and I tickle theirs back. I know I'm a hard person to love. I'm not a terrible person or anything, but I'm a runner. My fight or flight reactions are strongly seated in the flight column and most men don't seem to know what to do with that.

Sure, I've had a few one-night stands. They were all with the same person, but that still counts. He was my lab partner in my college Chemistry I class and used to make jokes about us having chemistry. Come to think of it, he was kind of a douchebag, but I was curious about sex and he wasn't terrible at it. Plus, the only time we saw each other was when we were studying so I didn't freak out very often. It worked for me, but I still wouldn't call it a relationship.

And at one point, Todd and I got drunk and decided if we weren't married by the time we were twenty-five, we'd marry each other. Seemed like a good idea at the time.

Then that quarter-life age was upon us, we looked at each other like the idea of being intimate made us both nauseous and never spoke of it again.

My experience with the opposite sex isn't much. More like almost none.

Maybe that's why I'm enjoying this time with Spencer. It's a whole new experience to have a man think I'm sexy and alluring. It's flattering when he comes up behind me just to put his arms around my waist and kiss my neck. And it feels oddly natural that he used the shower while I was at the vanity putting all my makeup on before tonight's signing.

Sure, we have two bathrooms since his continued travel good luck scored us adjoining rooms just like Austin. But Spencer made a point of using the same bathroom I was, just so we could talk while getting ready.

In a weird way, it kind of made me swoon. Plus, it kept me from getting distracted, which means we are right on time. For once.

Stepping out of the car at the bookstore where the event is being held, I'm surprised by the cold that pierces my skin. The weather in San Francisco is so strange. When you're in certain parts of the city, the sun feels warm. In other parts, there is a bone-chilling dampness in the air. And now that the sun is setting and the breeze off the ocean is stronger, it's definitely cooler. It's a good thing I wore my black leather pants, black leather jacket with a red tank top underneath, and a red bandana wrapped around my head. Not only am I playing the part of a pin-up girl loving author, the clothes hold my body heat in, while my red peep-toe heels give me a little bit of air conditioning on my feet.

Gotta love women's fashion.

"Did I tell you how amazing you look in those pants?" Spencer whispers in my ear as we walk toward the front door, his hand on my lower back. I love the feel of it.

Giggling, I smack him playfully on the chest. "Several times. Now hush. We have appearances to keep up."

He releases a resigned sigh and mutters, "Right. Appearances."

I know Spencer wants to come right out and let it be known that something is going on between us. Since we haven't defined our relationship, or friendship or whatever, I prefer keeping it private. As giddy as I am by where this seems to be going, I don't really think it's fair for anyone else to figure it out before we do. I've let my guard down with this small part of me. I'm taking baby steps. That's not unreasonable, right?

I don't have time to think much more about it when a man with shoulder length dark hair approaches us. His nametag says "Franklin," I assume he's an employee. At least I hope so. Otherwise it would be weird he's wearing a nametag.

"Good. You're here. Right on time. Are you ready?"

Somewhat taken aback by his directness, I stumble over my words. "Oh. Um. Yes. I guess so."

Franklin nods and turns to walk away. Spencer and I look at each other, shrug, and then hurry after the man, assuming we're to follow him. Sure enough, in a back corner of the room, there is a table set up for Spencer and me, and dozens of chairs are already filled with people.

When the audience sees us, the room erupts in cheers. Spencer raises his hand in a handsome and cool wave. I, on the other hand, curtsy which doesn't have quite the same effect because I'm wearing pants. And also because I stumble trying to stand back up from crossing my legs while wearing heels. This is something I should know better than to do. But of course, I don't.

Once again, thank goodness for Spencer's quick reaction time. Grabbing my elbow to steady me is much less embarrassing than faceplanting.

Standing behind a podium and microphone, I wait until Franklin gives me the go-ahead and begin my normal speech. The one about being so happy to be here, Spencer being a great guy, books being good to read, blah, blah, blah. Having done this so many times over the last couple of weeks, I can genuinely say my nerves are far steadier than they used to be.

Before I know it, it's time for the Q&A portion of the event.

Pointing to a reader who is exuding excitement, although I have yet to meet a reader who doesn't, she stands up, her smile bright.

"What made you decide to finally come out and let your readers know that Spencer is your muse?"

My hearts either stops or speeds up, I'm not really sure which one. She doesn't seem to notice, though.

"I mean, I guess it wasn't hard to figure out, ya know? The hair color, the eye color, the extreme sports. I feel like none of us are all that sharp since we didn't figure out, ya know?"

Laugher fills the room at her words, and I do my best to seem unaffected, but inside I'm a quivering mess.

What is she talking about? I never told anyone except Greer about Spencer. Well, and when Donna figured it out—

Wait.

Donna figured it out.

The Donna who has the same publisher as me and therefore the same publicist.

Dammit. This can't be happening.

Refusing to look at Spencer, who I am sure now thinks I am the biggest stalker out there, I try my hardest to play off the humiliation I feel. I need to clarify what she's talking about first.

"I mean, who isn't inspired when they watch Spencer Garrison skate. Am I right, ladies?" I smile and gesture to the man in question.

Amid the applause, "amens," and a few catcalls, I chance a look at him. He has the strangest look on his face. One that I don't want to try and decipher right now. Not when I'm feeling such abject humiliation and confirmation that it's best I don't get close to many people.

Still, it's not this woman's fault I'm having a breakdown in my head right now. I straighten my spine and push through a few more questions, all the while wanting to hide away and figure out what's going on.

"Okay, okay." Franklin eventually holds his hands up as he stands in front of the crowd. "We're gonna take a five-minute break before we start the signing part," he drones. "Make sure you have your ticket ready. We're going to line up in groups of twenty, so if you have one through twenty, line up. If you don't, you have to wait."

Ducking for cover behind one of the bookshelves where no one can see me, I clutch my hand to my heart.

This can't be happening. Donna didn't sell me out like that, did she? Why would she do such a thing?

"Aggi?" My eyes fly open to see Spencer standing in front of me, concern written all over his face and body language. "Shit. Sorry, I mean Adi. Are you okay?"

I nod once and reach my hand out. "Can I borrow your phone?" The words sound more like a whisper, and I'm surprised he can actually hear me.

But he never hesitates when he pulls it out of his pocket and places it in my shaking hands. "Of course. Did you forget yours?"

"It doesn't have what I need. I need—I need internet."

Thankfully, Franklin rounds the corner. "So, uh, the people are getting in line to sign your books, or whatever."

Licking my dry lips, I nod at him. "I need to make a quick pit stop. Is there a restroom I can use?"

"Uh, yeah, I guess." He points toward the back. "There's an employee area back there. When you go through the door it's on your right."

"Thank you."

Darting my way out from between the men, careful to not accidently brush up against the man I've been sleeping with but suddenly want to run away from, I ignore both of their stares. I need to figure out what is being said first. And maybe fire someone.

Oh, who am I kidding. I'd never fire someone. It's one of the reasons I still send paperback copies of my books to a friend who used to help me make graphics years ago. She doesn't do anything anymore and we haven't even spoken in a year, but I've never technically fired her, so I don't feel comfortable not paying her. It's a wonder I haven't been scammed into a pyramid scheme. I'm a prime target.

Finding the restroom, I lock the door behind me and quickly open Spencer's phone.

"Come on, come on, come on," I mutter as I clumsily find the internet app and figure out how to search for what I'm looking for. It takes a few minutes being that my fingers can't seem to touch the right buttons before the article comes up. Written by my publicist and put out into the world this morning.

New York Times Bestselling Author Adeline Snow is finally leveling with her fans as she reveals her highly secretive muse is none other than Spencer Garrison, the world-famous skateboarder she's on tour with.

I don't have to read further to know it only gets worse from there. I'm sure she made up quotes I never said and facts that never happened. "Maximum impact" is what she calls it. "Humiliation" is what I call it. One of my deepest darkest secrets wasn't hers to share. Hell, it wasn't Donna's to share and now it's out there for anyone and everyone to see. I'm living my own personal nightmare and battling my instinct to run away. I need to be alone to think and wrap my brain around the situation.

Leaning my head back against the door, I try to focus on my breathing as my thoughts swirl.

Is this why Spencer is with me? Did he know I had a crush on him and was just humoring me?

Does he think I'm a psycho now? Do all these people?

And how the hell am I supposed to push through my block when the only thing I want to do right now is quit my job, head to a deserted island, and spend the remainder of my days hiding and talking to a volleyball instead of people?

No. No, you're stronger than this Aggi. And you have fans who need you to hold it together. They deserve to meet the author they love.

Taking one last deep breath, I leave the safety of the unsterile and smelly room and walk out the door.

Regardless of how I feel and how this changes everything I thought I knew, I still have a job to do and people to see.

Putting on my game face, Adeline Snow comes out in full force, Aggi locked tightly away.

Chapter 22

Muse. Its not the first time someone has used that word in the time we've been together, but it's the first time someone literally pointed my way and said I was that inspiration for Aggi. That one strange little word sent my girl into a tizzy.

She tried to play it off like it didn't affect her, like me putting it all together wasn't making her heart race and her palms sweat. I saw the way her foot tapped behind the podium. I heard the quiver in her voice as she continued to smile and put her best Adeline Snow face forward. But, I also knew deep down she was plotting at least four different ways to run from me. From us. I just don't quite understand why.

I gave her the space she needed at the bookstore and assumed when we returned to our rooms, we'd climb into bed and I'd hold her while I told her none of it mattered. It's actually flattering to know she thought of me before we met. That she'd used my career as a basis for some of her most beloved characters. To know that these strong, dynamic men, "Heroes" as the book world calls them, were based on me is an ego boost like I've never had.

Instead, she asked for that space she'd mentioned before, walked into her room, and didn't unlock the adjoining door again. After a fitful sleep, I rose before the sun and went down to the hotel gym for a workout. My knee hasn't bothered me much on this tour but the damp air in San Francisco has brought on the ache I remember. Pushing myself more than I should, I'll likely regret the run on the treadmill later on the plane.

As I approach my door, I contemplate knocking on Aggi's door instead. I need to know she's okay. To kiss her and hold her and make sure she knows nothing has changed. I like her, and she likes me. That's all that matters right now. The rest is just publicity and bullshit her publicist, and probably Freddy, put out into the world to build more buzz.

I don't knock. I promised her I'd respect her need for space and I need to honor that. Instead, I slide my card in front of the lock to my door and am surprised when I walk in and Aggi is standing in my room.

"Sweetheart." The relief I feel in seeing her in my room evident in the way I whisper the nickname I prefer.

"Sorry. I, I needed to get my makeup from your bathroom. I will be ready to leave in about thirty if that works for you."

"Honey, we have to talk about this."

"Spencer, I need to get ready. Thirty, okay?"

Nodding, I watch as she walks through the door to

her room and flinch when the door locks. She's locking me out of the room. Out of her life. Or so she thinks. If she thinks I'm just going to walk away because she's a little embarrassed, she has another thing coming. More than ever, I'm determined to win this woman's heart.

•••

"Mr. Garrison, here are your tickets. I'm sorry for the confusion on the upgrade."

"No problem, things happen." Handing the woman at the counter my credit card, I pause when I hear a gasp behind me.

"You? You're the one paying for the upgrades to first class?"

For a split second I consider coming up with a bullshit excuse, like I'm using Freddy's credit card. But after everything that has happened, with every-thing she's feeling, I know now more than ever she needs me to be honest with her. "I am."

"Spencer."

"What? It's no biggie. I need the leg room and you need the rest. First class seats are much more comfort-able for naps."

"Stop!" Aggi shouts slamming her hand on the counter, startling the poor attendant. "Please don't up-grade my ticket."

"Aggi, baby, come on. It's not a big deal."

Hand in my face, she turns her attention to the woman at the desk. "I would like to stay in coach, please."

The clerk nods in response and glances to me for confirmation. What am I supposed to do? Go all alpha male and override what Aggi has asked? No. That's not me and if I know anything about my girl, it's that she doesn't like that alpha shit anyway. Well, except in bed, but even that may be pushing it a little.

Satisfied with winning this round, Aggi takes her ticket from the very quiet attendant and spins on her heel, making her way toward security. Grabbing my new upgraded ticket I walk quickly to catch up to Aggi, frustrated because in the confusion I never bothered to make sure I was being placed in coach as well. It doesn't go unnoticed that instead of her normal Aggi travelwear of leggings and a flowy top and next to no makeup with her glasses on, today she's made up as Adeline Snow. Full makeup. Coifed hair. Leather pants and heels to match.

Full armor.

Stepping in line, I reach for her hand, but she responds by gripping the strap of her crossbody, not allowing me any contact. She's punishing me for something I didn't do. For something I don't even care about. This is not okay with me, and I'm starting to get pissed.

When we finally make it through security and walk toward our gate, I glance at my phone and see I have a few more text messages from my sister and Freddy. Kate claims to have had a gag reflex over her favorite sex scenes when she realized she was basically reading about me in the bedroom but got over it pretty quick. Now she is over the moon knowing I've been connected to her favorite books and insists this is more proof that Aggi, or Adi as she knows her, is meant to be her new best friend and the mother of my future children. How she reaches these conclusions is beyond me, hence the ignoring of her messages.

Freddy, on the other hand, wants to build off this development and is trying to convince me to write a book. A fucking book about what, I have no idea. He seemed surprised when I told him unequivocally no.

Taking the seat next to her, I set my backpack down and turn to Aggi. She shifts, and I think for a minute she's going to leave but when she doesn't I have a glimmer of hope we'll get past this.

"Talk to me."

"What is there to say? Thanks? Thanks for letting me think our upgrades were a perk of this tour and how foolish I looked for weeks commenting on that? Or surprise! You're my muse. It's not humiliating at all for you to know, for the entire world to know that you were the inspiration for some of my bestselling books. Books I can't seem to write anymore. Since I actually met you I haven't written a word because writing you after actually knowing you, after we . . . well, you know, I can't write. I'm broken." Her last words are whispered as she sniffles, and I know she's going to cry.

Instinctively, I pull her to me, nestling her head into my chest, rubbing my hand down her back as I place a kiss to the top of her head. Her sniffles go on for a few minutes but when she lifts her hand to wipe away the fallen tears, I let her pull away from me.

"Sorry. Crap, I think you may need to change your shirt." Looking down to where she's pointing, I see a wet spot on my shirt where she was resting her head and shrug.

"Feel better?" She nods once so I continue. "Why are you dressed like Adeline Snow?"

"What?"

"You aren't dressed like you. This is Adeline. Why?"

She diverts her gaze, and I know it's one more wall that has just gone up. "I have to, Spencer. Everyone knows what a fraud I am. You have no idea how embarrassing this is."

"You've lost me, sweetheart. You are a lot of things, but a fraud isn't one of them. You have nothing to be embarrassed about. I'm sorry about the upgrades. I wanted us to have time together, and I knew you'd argue about me paying so I didn't offer up the facts when you assumed it was part of the tour."

Grabbing her hand, I link our fingers and lift her hand to my lips, kissing it twice. "Aggi, I like you, and I'm pretty sure you like me back. Nothing has changed for me except my admiration for your career and professionalism. You handled last night like a champ and I was, I *am*, so proud of you."

Her eyes snap up to mine and for a second I think I may have gotten through to her. "You were, *are*?"

"Yeah, baby. I just want to move on from this. Will you let this go and let us keep being us? When we're together, it's just Aggi and Spencer. Adeline Snow is for the masses but you're just for me. Can we do that?"

She bites her lip and I realize I'm not making as much headway as I thought. "I don't know Spencer. I'm really raw right now. I need time. I know you don't get it. And I'm trying to figure out how to explain it but"—she bangs her fist gently to her forehead, eyes shut tightly—"this damn writer's block won't let me put the words together to explain. My emotions are all over the place, and I need to process it all."

Her frustration with herself is palpable and my immediate thought is to not make it worse. "I have no problem giving you time to sort it all out. I understand." She breathes a sigh of relief so I try one last time. "But can I at least ask about putting you in the seat next to me in first class?"

"I think I'd prefer to do this short flight in the cheap seats if you don't mind."

My heart sinks. "You need space too."

Nodding, she offers me the slightest of smiles. It looks sad almost and while I want to keep holding on to hope, it's quickly fading away. Aggi slips her hand from mine and pulls out her laptop, tapping the keys a few times before staring at the screen, her bottom lip tugged between her teeth.

Tension radiates off her and I need to lighten the mood. "I think we have a full day with zero commitments for the tour when we get to LA; do you have plans?"

"Writing. I'm so far behind on my deadline."

"Do you think you can block out a little time for

me?"

Her teeth tug on her bottom lip as she decides if it's worth it or not. Finally, she nods. "Of course."

Breathing an audible sigh of relief I respond with, "Good. I have a surprise for you. I think it may help this block you've stumbled behind."

"Well, it can't hurt at this point," she grumbles as she pulls her headphones from her bag and slowly places them on her ears as she begins tapping on the keys of her laptop before we begin boarding.

Separately.

Chapter 23

Aggi

Final Stop: Los Angeles
Home of the Summer X Games, circa 2003 – 2013

As much as I missed sitting next to him on that plane, I needed some distance from Spencer. When I'm near him, I can't breathe. That's always been true, but especially now that my emotions are so out of control.

I tried to spend the flight writing, which I'm sure thrilled my rowmates to no end. Especially since I was stuck in the middle due to our seat assignment snafu at check-in. After dropping my bag on the foot of the man to the left of me and accidentally elbowing the woman on the right, I finally got my laptop open and myself situated.

And then I stared at a blank screen for the next hour.

I should have known better than to try. I'm too off kilter.

I know Spencer feels it. He's become quite astute when it comes to my emotions. And therein lies part of the problem. He's figuring out too much too fast, and I already know how this ends. He will get tired of my oddities and decide I'm too much effort, leaving me heartbroken and possibly unable to recover.

I know my thoughts sound self-depreciating but they're really not. One of the curses of being a people watcher is I can spot patterns of behavior a mile away. I know Spencer likes me, but fear has thrown me back to all my original concerns. I'm no longer convinced he likes me *enough*. It's one thing to enjoy my quirky personality. It's a completely different thing to have your deepest darkest fantasies and desires spread open before him like, well like all of my books.

That's the part about my writing that no one except Greer has ever known. Every single one of the words I put down on paper for the world to read are actual emotions I feel. Real fantasies I have. They are the truest part of my soul. Eventually I would have trusted Spencer with that information. But I needed to feel confident he would take that information and treat it with kid gloves. Now I'm not sure if he's humoring me with all his sweet words, or if he understands the gravity of this personal information at all.

Either it is hurtful or humiliating and a huge blow to my already wishy-washy ego.

So I appreciate the silence he's afforded me on our drive out of Los Angeles. I still don't know where we're headed, but watching the landscape as we get there makes it worth it no matter what.

California has always intrigued me. As a Midwesterner, born and raised, the West Coast has always seemed magical and exciting. The few times I've visited have not been disappointing. Even now, seeing mountains in the background of a vibrant metropolis makes my heart race.

Inspired, however, I am not.

Pulling into a more residential area, my curiosity finally gets the best of me.

"Where are we?"

Turning on the blinker, he looks both ways before pulling onto a side street. "We're almost there."

A few minutes later we pull into a small parking lot and I gasp.

The Skateboarding Hall of Fame. He brought me to the freaking mecca of skateboarding.

"Wow." That's all the only coherent word that comes out of my mouth as I look up at the building. All of my favorites are here as inductees: Gregg Weaver and Eric Dressen and Tony Hawk. For the first time in a couple days, my excitement level is rising.

Pulling the car into the space, Spencer parks and turns to face me. "Aggi, I've spent the last three weeks in your world getting to know who you are. Not just the world-famous author, but the person. I want you to know me too."

His words hit me harder than I realized they would. I thought I did know him. Having spent time in his home, the one he designed, showed me so much of who he is. But, to hear this, to hear him say he wants to show me more—I'm not sure if I'm flattered or feel stupid for letting things get as far as they have when maybe I didn't know him very well at all.

But I also know after tonight's signing, we're heading our separate ways and going home. Call me selfish or stupid, but I want this time with him as Aggi and Spencer. Who knows if I'll ever have this opportunity or will ever see him again. Despite my reservations, I respond by unclicking my seatbelt and opening the car door.

He follows suit and in just a few minutes we're inside what I can confidently call my version of Disneyland.

"Holy shit, Spencer. Look at all those boards!" I exclaim, blown away by the sheer beauty of every design and style a skater could imagine. They're everywhere. Hanging from a chain link fence from bottom to top. Attached to the ceiling. There are hundreds of them. Maybe thousands.

Immediately, I pull out my camera and begin clicking. Zooming in and back out. Turning every which way to try and capture the beauty of the colors and shapes. It's stunning.

As we wander around the museum, Spencer points out a few interesting pieces like a 1970 Powell Honeycomb Quicksilver prototype. Supposedly there are only two of these in the world and here I am, up close and personal with one of them.

Un. Real.

Tearing my eyes away from the rarity, I look behind me and freeze. Right across the aisle is a picture of the woman who introduced me to the love of skateboarding. Kim Cespedes was one of the first women in the 70s to focus on bowls and pipes and tricks. Most women during that era performed freestyle and choreographed gymnastics routines on the board. Not Kim. She not only held her own with the men, she smoked them, even doing backside airs in pools only a year after they were unveiled by "the boys."

And if I take a few steps and reach out, I can touch her board.

"Amazing, right?"

I look up at Spencer, who is smiling down at me, obviously delighted I'm enjoying this so much.

"Spencer, I just . . . this is . . . I can't even explain how I'm feeling."

"Well, lookie there," he jokes. "The writer has lost her words."

I grimace, and he quickly realizes what he just said.

"Sorry. I didn't mean it that way. I'll wait until you're unblocked to joke about you being rendered speechless again."

Now I feel bad. "No, don't be sorry. I'm just—I'm hypersensitive right now. Don't worry about it."

He clears his throat and shoves his hands in his pockets. I've clearly made the situation uncomfortable again, which makes me want to kick myself. He doesn't let the silence linger for long. "Anyway, not many people know this, in fact I don't think anyone does. But my dream, I guess fantasy would be a better explanation, is to have my picture and board hanging right in this area."

"You want to be an inductee?"

He shrugs. "Don't we all? I can't tell you how many times I've made up scenarios in my head about what I would say in my speech and what Maxim cover model would accompany me." I quirk an eyebrow at him, making him chuckle. "Don't look at me like that. I was a kid and the Maxim magazine was my dad's. Every pubescent kid on the tour wanted to claim Jennifer Love Hewitt as his own. I grew out of that. Now I just think about the speech."

"I have no doubt your picture and board will be hanging in here someday. You've won how many gold medals already?"

"But that's not why this is my dream. I want to leave a lasting impression in this sport because of the work I do with kids. Because of the work I do in communities around the country. I don't want to be known as the guy who could ride a skateboard really well. I want to be known as the guy who made a difference in the world."

"That's really important to you, isn't it?"

He shrugs. "I remember what it was like to not have a dad around. It wasn't his fault. Divorce just is what it is, and California is where my mother's family was. She wouldn't have made it if it weren't for their support. I get that. But that doesn't mean it didn't hurt that he wasn't there."

I listen intently, knowing he is sharing a deep part of his soul with me.

"Skateboarding saved me. Pushing my body to

gain the height I need to do a one eighty or whatever, it was an outlet for my anger. There were men there who cheered me on and told me I was special. It was so much more important than I ever let on and I know there are so many other kids out there who need it too. So no. I don't want to be considered a Hall of Famer yet. I have too much of a difference to make first. And now, with retirement hanging over my head, I'm terrified I won't leave the kind of mark I want. That my name will fade and with it, opportunities to keep doing the rest."

There's not much I can say to validate his concerns, so I blurt out the only thing I can think of. "I believe in you."

His eyes find mine and he holds my gaze. "I know you do, Aggi. I think you believe in me in a way no one else does. You see all of me," he says softly.

The words give me pause and I want to trust his feelings. I really do. But my insecurities are still roaring in my head, making it hard to figure out what to do. I'm confused and afraid and still frustrated with this damn block.

When I say nothing, he continues, "You've written a piece of me into so many of your stories, I don't think you realized how accurate you were." Offering a small smile, I break his stare and pull my camera back up to my face, so I can hide behind my picture taking. Armor back up.

Chapter 24

Spencer

Tonight is the last stop on the promotional tour, and I've decided to put a little more effort into my look. Sure, this is California and if there is the spot that would grant me the grace to dress down it's here. I could easily throw on a T-shirt and shorts and call it a day. But, it may also be the last night I'm going to spend with Aggi, and I'd be lying if I said I didn't hold some hope for more photo opportunities and a chance to wrap my arms around her. I saw the way she looked at me the last time I put in the extra effort, and I'm not too macho to admit I liked it. A lot. So a pair of dark wash jeans and a white button-up shirt it is. Gone are my Vans and in their place are a pair of dress shoes I had to dig into the back of my closet for.

As I roll the sleeves of my shirt up, I think back to our day. A day I thought would have her telling me she chooses me. Us. I mistakenly thought taking her to the Hall of Fame and showing another piece of my life, of my dreams, she'd realize everything I've said is true. I care for her. I like her. Hell, I'm falling for her.

For a few hours, I thought we were putting all the muse business behind us. She laughed and let me lead her around, her hand in mine. Then we headed to one of my favorite taco joints for a late lunch and all the progress we'd made slowly unraveled.

I don't know what changed between the Hall of Fame and lunch, but she slowly replaced the carefree Aggi with the armor she holds onto so tightly. Gone was the carefree and joking Aggi, replaced with the quiet and professional Adeline Snow.

I didn't dare tell her about my call with Freddy when she was in the restroom cleaning up the epic salsa spill from her pants. It turns out the muse outing has had quite the buzz on social media. Some fans have even created fan pages referring to us as "Spendeline" whatever that means. Freddy said the publicists are falling over themselves with the positive response and while they aren't encouraging the rumors that Aggi, I mean Adeline, and I are a couple, they also aren't putting those same rumors to rest. Something I've made sure to let Freddy know he'd better handle. If I thought I was losing Aggi with the outing, having this shit all over the internet is sure to send her running for the hills. Thank God for her antiquated flip phone and inability to check social media hourly.

Grabbing my keys and a couple of bottles of water from the refrigerator, I exit my condo. There are perks to having a place in California. I get to use my own shower, drive my own car, and sleep in my own bed. A bed I hope I can convince Aggi to spend her last night in.

The downside, however, is there are no guarantees I'll be sleeping next to my girl tonight. Not in the same bed or even in the room next door. Had I known we would have gotten this close when the tour started, I would have demanded to stay in the hotel with her. Unfortunately, my lack of foresight means it's booked now.

The drive to her hotel doesn't take me long since I've bypassed the freeway for side streets. This traffic reminds me of one of the reasons I chose to build my house in Lexington and not here. Settling into the plush leather seat, I let my mind drift to my decision about the future. I haven't talked it out with Kate like I usually do, but I'm pretty sure I know exactly what I'm going to do.

•••

"What is this?"

"Well, Agnes, this is a BMW Seven Series. Her name is Lola."

A cross between a laugh, scoff, and cough rolls from her. "Lola?"

"Yep. I wanted to name her Lolita, but Kate said it sounded too . . . dark romance. Whatever that means."

"It's a subgenre." Her response is quiet as she approaches the car cautiously.

"It's a car, sweetheart. You don't have to be so timid."

"Spencer, this is a far cry from your truck."

Shrugging, I open the passenger door and watch as

she slowly lowers herself into the leather seat. A small moan of appreciation for the soft leather escapes her and sends a shot of lust below my belt. She already stole my breath when she walked out with her long brown hair in soft waves, one side pinned back while the other hangs across her chest. The dress she chose is a beautiful shade of purple that sets off her skin tone perfectly. Hitting just above the knee, it accentuates her legs and draws attention to the high heels she's wearing with her painted toes peeking out.

As I settle behind the wheel, I look to my right as she runs her finger lightly over the console. "You look beautiful, Aggi." Slowly, she turns her head and gives me one of her true smiles as a thank you.

For the next twenty minutes, we don't speak. We sit in silence, each of us likely pondering the same question. What happens after tonight? I know Aggi, and she's going to make an excuse and run away from me. She's going to pretend what we've shared these past few weeks was no more than a new friendship with a few perks. She'll lie and promise to keep in touch, and that'll be the end of Aggi and Spencer.

As much as it pains me to think of that happening, a piece of me knows if I push the issue, I won't draw her to me. I'll only push her farther away. I want nothing more than to lay my feelings out for her like a buffet and welcome her to take it all, to stay with me here a little longer and work through all of this. Together we will figure out where we're going and how we make this work. I want her nights in my bed and her days finding inspiration for her books. Yet, I know that won't work with my girl. She needs to figure this out on her own. At her own pace.

The signing goes off without a hitch. The readers there to see Aggi are eager and over-the-top excited. You'd think the Hemsworth we met in Aspen was here. Nope, it's just Adeline Snow. Gracious and patient as always, Aggi speaks to each reader with undivided attention and I, once again, watch in awe. Different from other events we've attended on this tour is the line I have for autographs and photos. As I'd hoped, a few of the fans have asked for pictures with both Aggi and me, and I've been able to wrap my arm around her, even if only for a few seconds. Each time my hand has slid behind her back, slower than necessary, I've felt the shivers and heard the small intakes of breath and every time, I've smiled huge for the camera. Even better, I'd gotten to catch her when she's stumbled more than once. I'm allowing myself to be convinced her nerves are about letting me go. Gotta stroke my own ego somehow.

When the last fan hugs Aggi and thanks her for bringing the sexy back to her bedroom and into her marriage, I choke a little on my water. Aggi looks like she's seen a ghost. An expression of horror crosses her face before she recovers like the professional she is with a simple thank you. But then a hint of Aggi instead of Adeline appears when she shouts "Godspeed" like the woman is headed out on a mission.

"Did that woman just thank you for her sex life?" I ask with a chuckle.

She furrows her brow, still tracking the woman

as she walks out the front door. "I think she did. I've never had that happen before. Usually Donna or one of the other authors who write the sexier books gets that response."

Taking her chin between my thumb and forefinger, I turn her to face me. "I know from personal experience you have every right to receive the thanks that woman gave, baby."

Slowly a pink hue covers Aggi's face and she buries her face in her hands and groans. "Spencer! You cannot say things like that."

Shrugging I say, "It's true, sweetheart. You're a sexy woman and should own it." Blinking her eyes at rapid pace, the pink hue turns a light crimson, and I laugh as I pull my keys from my pocket and toss them in the air before catching them. "Ready?"

Nodding, Aggi grabs her bag before walking to the manager and thanking her for a flawless event. As we approach my car, I contemplate asking if she wants to grab a bite to eat or a drink. I don't want the night to end, but I also know eventually it will.

"What time is your flight in the morning?"

"Eight. I scheduled a car for five thirty. It's going to be an early morning for me."

"Sounds like it. I can still take you if you want, the offer stands."

She smiles shyly, and I already know what her answer is going to be. "I appreciate it, but the car is fine. It's too early, I'd hate for you to drive all the way back here to take me."

"You could come home with me." It slips out before I can stop it.

"Spencer," she says quietly and with resolve.

I already knew what her answer would be, but hearing her say it makes me feel like I've been punched in the gut again.

"I know, Aggi. I know."

The rest of the drive to the hotel is quiet. Gone is the comfortable silence I've been accustomed to with Aggi, and in its place is tension. Instead of pulling up to the front doors to let her out, I park in short-term parking and kill the engine. Quickly, I exit the car and run around to open her door before extending my hand to her. With only a slight hesitation, she places her tiny hand in mine and stands from the car. I don't let go of her hand as I walk us through the large front doors of the hotel and straight to the elevators.

I spy a small group of people talking animatedly near the elevators. I slow our pace before speaking. "Are you sure I can't convince you to stay a few more days?"

Shaking her head Aggi tugs her bottom lip between her teeth and looks at the ground as we continue to walk. The elevator opens and the group boards, a gentleman placing his hand on the door to hold it for us. I wave him off, needing this time with Aggi. When the doors close, I step up and push the up arrow before turning to face the woman who looks like she's moments from losing a battle with herself.

"I hoped we'd have this conversation in a more private setting but here it goes. I like you, Aggi. You bring something out in me I haven't felt in a long time. I want us to spend more time together, get to know each other better. Not the athlete and the author but the people we are deep down." Cupping her face in my hands, I force her gaze up to mine hoping she can see the honesty in my words. "I want to know the girl who stumbles and apologizes to pieces of furniture. I want to listen to you tell me story after story and watch as your eyes light up because being a storyteller is your passion. Having you in my bed is a perk and seeing you in those damn footy pajamas you have in your luggage is a sight I want morning after morning." Her eyes widen at my mention of the pajamas she probably didn't realize I saw in her bags. "I'm not asking you to give up your life, Aggi, I just want to be part of it."

She moves her hand quickly to brush her cheek, breaking our physical connection and forcing me to shift backward.

"The thing is, I can't make you want the same from me. I wish I could, God how I wish I could. This is me telling you I'm here. The ball is in your court."

No longer hiding her tears, she sniffles as her hand falls from mine and she places both of her hands on my waist. Stepping forward, I place a kiss to the top of her head before turning and walking away.

Chapter 25

Aggi

I miss him.

There. I said it. I admitted to myself that I. Miss. Spencer.

To be honest, it's not a huge surprise I feel this way. What is a surprise, however, is the intensity with which I'm feeling it. It isn't like missing my mom because I haven't talked to her in a while, or missing Todd because I need my friend fix.

Nope. This is like missing an arm. Or at least I assume this is what missing an arm feels like. Minus the phantom limb pain, the relearning of daily tasks, the surgeries—

Okay it's nothing like missing an arm. No, it's like missing a part of my soul. And that has me spooked because I think I may have fallen for him. A little. Not fully and completely, because we've only known each other for such a short time. Regardless of how much time we spent talking, laughing, and making love, it would be impossible to have feelings that deep for him yet.

Right?

Sighing, I push my laptop away again. For the last two days, all I've done is mechanically throw words on a page, hoping it sorts itself out and makes some sort of sense. I'm not holding my breath, though. Mostly my thoughts have been about the look on Spencer's face when he walked away from me, and the expression was the opposite of romance. It was defeat. Like our happily ever after was never going to happen.

He looked so sad, yet so resolved at the same time. Like he wanted to say more. Wanted to beg me to reconsider staying with him. For a split second, I actually did. When his hands cupped my face and he made sure I could see straight inside to his soul as he bared his deepest feelings to me, I almost said yes. I almost jumped up, wrapped my legs around him, and kissed him with as much gusto as I could.

I wanted to. God, how I wanted to. But then I realized I would likely throw us off balance and we'd end up in a heap on the floor. I remembered all the people around, and the fear the fall would end up going viral overwhelmed me. The memory of that stupid article that ruined everything crossed my mind again, and I just couldn't do it. I couldn't muster the confidence to tell him I felt the same way and I trusted him to not hurt me. Not when every nuance and similarity of him and his life were pulled out of my stories and presented to the world like factual evidence on a platter.

So I let him walk away, taking my heart with him.

I never knew my publicist paid attention to the details of my books but oh boy did she. The initial article and the posts by my readers and Spencer's fans that followed listed them one by one, each highlighting with quotes, photos, and real-life moments as further proof of his role in my stories. It was like seeing my naked body being presented to the world and every freckle pointed out individually. Exposing every fantasy and moment for the world to see private parts of me I never chose to share with anyone.

Dramatic, much, Aggi? I guess those intense feelings and emotions are why I'm paid to do this job.

I'm not a huge crier. But that night, I sobbed. I didn't even order room service. Just put on my favorite footie pajamas, crawled under the covers, and wept for the hurt on Spencer's face. For the hurt in my own heart. I cried until I fell asleep, knowing my black rimmed glasses would camouflage a night of emotions anyway. The next morning, I dragged myself out of bed at five a.m., with just enough time to brush my teeth, cram everything in my suitcase, and make it to my Uber on time.

Of course, with my puffy eyes not working all that well, I ended up zipping a sock up in the teeth of the suitcase and had to fight with it to let go. Thank goodness the Uber driver was running a few minutes late like I was.

My eyes glance up at my laptop when my instant messenger dings. Donna's trying to reach me.

Taking a deep breath, I have to decide if I want to talk to her or not. I still feel betrayed. She never should have told anyone anything about me without my permission. It's not okay, and I'm not sure if our friendship will recover.

Clicking my fingernails on my desk a few times as I figure out what to do, I finally decide to take the bull by the horns and open the message. Even if I don't trust Donna, she's still a colleague and will be for the foreseeable future. I have to be able to work with her. And maybe explaining how much she hurt me will help this feeling of despair inside me start to heal.

Donna: How was the tour? You look like you had so much fun and those pictures with Spencer were adorable!

Of course she thinks so. That was the point of the article, wasn't it? To put attention on "how cute" we were?

Me: It was nerve-wracking and did nothing to help my block. But at least it's over.

Donna: But you're still going to see Spencer, right? I've been rooting for you!

Me: No, I'm not still seeing Spencer. As you, and everyone else in the country now know, he's my muse and nothing more.

It takes her a few minutes to respond and I know it's because I sound snippy. I could pretend my tone is coming across wrong, but I don't have enough emotional energy to care. Finally, a message pops up.

Donna: But you guys were smiling so hard at the X Games. And at the Skateboarding Hall of Fame.

Oh good. More pictures taken when we weren't looking.

Donna: Did something happen?

My fingertips rub my forehead. I suddenly have a headache coming on. How does she not get it? How does no one get it?

Thinking about my answer, I finally decide to tell the honest truth, no matter how hard it is.

*Me: Yes, something happened. Our publicists found out Spencer has been my muse for all these years, told the entire book/extreme sports community, and every secret fantasy and thought I've ever had was just handed over to the one person who hadn't earned that information from me yet. That was *my* information to share. And because of it, anything that was or wasn't beginning to develop imploded before it had a chance to begin.*

There. I said it. For the first time, maybe ever, I let someone besides Todd and my mother feel the brunt of my anger. Maybe brunt is giving myself too much credit. More like a nudge. But it's still more than Donna has ever seen before.

Once again, her reply isn't immediate. But when it comes through it makes me groan.

Donna: Answer your phone. I'm calling you now.

Dropping my head on my desk, I take deep, yoga breaths as I wait. Expressing my anger over the internet is one thing. Actually making the words come from my mouth is completely different.

This is what I get for not just letting this go.

Glaring at my phone when it finally rings, I wait until the last second to answer.

"Hello?" I squeak out.

"I have two things to say and I want you to hear me out," she demands.

This isn't going to be good.

"First of all, I have never, ever heard you speak in such a harsh tone. I know it's because you are hurting." Grimacing, I open my mouth to blurt out an apology, but she cuts me off before anything comes out. "And I am so damn proud of you for speaking up."

Errrr . . . What?

"Adeline, this is the first time you have trusted me enough to level with me about how you feel. I know sharing your feelings is hard and I feel really honored."

Huh. I was not expecting that.

"But I also want to clear something up because I know what you were implying."

I grimace again, that same apology once again on the tip of my tongue as I anticipate what she's about to say: It's not a big deal, it's good marketing, the only one who cares is you, blah, blah, blah.

"Honey, I didn't tell anyone your secret."

And the soundtrack in my head screeches to a stop again. Seriously. How does she keep surprising me?

Sitting up straight, I push the hair out of my face. "Donna, you're the only one who knew. Well, you and my editor, but she doesn't even know our publicists or work with the publisher."

"I can see why you would assume it was me—"

"Which makes an ass out of you and me," I interrupt with an inappropriately timed giggle.

"Stop that," she chides. "You didn't make an ass out of anyone. It was a valid assumption. But I'm telling you, I never breathed a word. I wouldn't do that to you. Or anyone. You know my latest book? Tales of a Boudoir Fantasy?"

"I haven't read it yet."

"No worries. You're busy. My point is, the entire book is a fantasy I've had for years about the guy I loved in high school. The whole thing is based on him and my deepest, darkest thoughts I have on what could have been if he hadn't moved away the middle of our senior year. I'm still not over that, by the way."

Her admission kind of makes me sad. "Wait. Stop. Why haven't you tracked him down? It's the age of social media. Maybe you can reconnect."

She sighs. "I already did. He's happily married with a few kids." My heart sinks for the loss of something she never had. For a romance lover, this is not the way the story is supposed to go. "And before you say it, there is no 'maybe someday' about it. I loved him enough then, and maybe still do now, that I would never wish ill on him or his wife."

Wow. Her words blow me away. To love someone enough that you wish nothing but happiness for them, even if you have to walk away because it won't be with you, is the most selfless kind of love someone can have.

It's what Spencer did when he walked away from me.

I know he was truthful when he said he doesn't want to push if I don't want him. But I also know he let me go because it's what I needed in that moment. He knows me well enough to know that pushing me to a decision then would have caused more distress. Time alone is the only way I can sort out my thoughts and feelings even if I miss him every minute of that time to myself.

He let me go because he has a selfless kind of love for me. Or like, anyway. The love will come later, but only if I let it.

"My point is," Donna says, interrupting my giant epiphany. "I wouldn't want that former love of my life to know the book is about him any more than you wanted Spencer to know. I get it. It's why I never, ever, planned to breathe a word about it to anyone."

I blink a few times as I have another epiphany. *What is it with these giant realizations today?*

"So what you're saying is, they made the story up."

"That would be my guess, yes."

"His publicist and my publicist got together and made up a story about my feelings and blasted it for the world to see only to garner attention?"

"Wouldn't be the first time," Donna reminds me. "Fans have been asking about who your muse is for years. I'd be willing to bet they decided this was the perfect opportunity to use that lingering secret to their advantage. Even if they had to fudge the information a little, or a lot they didn't really know, and to them it didn't really matter. This made for a great story."

"And I confirmed it all by my reaction." Dropping my head onto my desk with a thud, I'm not sure which hurts more: my forehead or my pride.

She gives me a minute to take a few deep breathes and pull my thoughts together before she finally levels with me completely. "I have a bad feeling you are about to tell me you saw the article, overreacted, and pushed away the first man who has ever gotten your motor revving. Am I right?"

"Maybe?"

She snorts a laugh. "Also known as yes. Look Adi, I've known you for a long time. And yes, it has been all on-line and at signings. But even from the pictures, you were so at ease with him. I've never seen you look so comfortable in your own skin. Is that something you want to explore further?"

Nailed it.

"Yes."

"Then what are you waiting for?"

"To feel confident enough to go for it?"

She huffs in frustration, and I can practically hear her throwing her hands up in exasperation. "Adi, I know you think you're clumsy and quirky. Those aren't terrible qualities; they're endearing. But you are also smart and funny and kind. You are dynamic. And I have news for you. As awesome as Spencer Garrison is, and yes, he is one hot piece of ass, he is also a man. That means he farts on demand, stinks up the bathroom, and probably leaves dirty underwear on the floor." An unattractive snort comes out of me as she makes me laugh. "He probably forgets his mama's birthday and flicks boogers when he thinks no one is looking. Because that's what men do. And you're laughing because it's true."

"He did fart in his sleep one night when we were together. I never told him, but I thought something had died until I realized what it was."

"Well, there ya go. He's not as perfect as you like to pretend his is. Also, I wish I could fist-bump you for tapping that."

My giggles take over, and it feels good to laugh. Really good. Like a weight has been lifted off my shoulders. Not because I wasn't betrayed by my friend, but because I somehow know she's right. Spencer isn't any more perfect than I am, but I like him anyway. Can't the same be true for him?

The conclusions I've drawn up are not about anything Spencer has done. Hell, the assumptions I made were not about anything Donna has ever done. They're all about me and my own self-sabotage. Why I do it, well, that's a question for another day and possibly for a future therapist to figure out. But I have a more immediate problem—how to let Spencer know I need him, and I'm ready to dive into this thing head first. Even if it scares me. Or I break my neck at the bottom of the pool.

And just like that, an idea hits me out of nowhere. With my brain spinning, I have to get off the phone. Now.

"Um, Donna, I don't mean to be rude, but the writing fog hit me. I think the block is busted."

She gasps. "Ohmygod, go! Don't stay on the phone! Get those words down!"

I don't even say goodbye, just flip my phone shut and grab my laptop.

The idea pours out of me and I write.

And I write.

And I write.

And two days later, Greer has all of her thirty thousand words with more on the way.

Chapter 26

Spencer

One month later

I've become accustomed to sunrises in Lexington. Watching them alone has sucked, but there doesn't seem to be much I can do about that. Kate has called me a borderline stalker for the amount of time I've spent online following Aggi's alter ego. Adeline Snow has enjoyed quite a bit of coffee, her socks have been making appearances on Sunday, and if her hashtags are any indication, she found her words again. I'm proud of her and have typed out more than one text to her with just those words only to delete them.

Time. I promised myself I'd give her time. But I didn't think she'd really need it. I assumed over these last few weeks she'd at least reach out to me, tag me in a post, comment on one of my posts. Crickets. That's what I've found instead. Using my sister for intel wasn't easy, so I was forced to come clean with her. The day I admitted my feelings for Aggi or as she knows her, Adeline, I think I may have lost some of my hearing.

Kate assured me that Adeline has been active in her reader group but only to update on the progress of her new book. She's keeping the premise under wraps but promised it's going to be the most epic of love stories and the hero is the swooniest of all her leading men. Kate's words, not mine. And, if I know my girl, not hers either.

The idea that I may be the inspiration for any new character she creates has me a little on edge. And, inspired. I realized if Aggi is writing and planning to publish her book after the whole muse-gate fiasco, then I need to take her lead and handle my own shit.

I've officially announced my retirement. I promised to fulfill my commitments over the next year but by next summer I want to be spending more of my time with my foundation and traveling the country speaking to and working with kids. I've even brought on a new marketing person/creative director who is looking to expand our programs to include a new focus on children with special needs.

Rising from my seat on the patio, I take my coffee cup to the sink and rinse it before placing it in the dishwasher. A quick look at the clock on the fridge, and I decide it's a reasonable enough time to call my sister. She has a few rugrats who have probably had her up and wishing it was happy hour for at least an hour.

Tapping Kate's contact, I tread down the hall to the office just as she answers the phone. "Come take these hellions, please."

"Is that anyway to talk about your precious babies?"

"Yes, I birthed them. I can call them what I like. Seriously, please come visit and be uncle of the year for at least three days. Reed and I need a break."

"Depends on what kind of intel you have for me." Kate begins to respond with what I'm sure is a smartass remark but a crash and a scream in the background distracts her.

"I swear these kids are sending me to an early grave. I have to go, there's syrup everywhere and your niece thinks she can make syrup angels like snow angels. I'll call you back."

You'd think calls like this would be instant birth control for me. They aren't. If anything, it makes me want a family more than before. I just hope whatever gene the kids inherited to act like monkeys in the zoo is from Reed's family and not ours.

Looking up at the pictures on my credenza, one of which is Kate and me at an actual zoo as kids, I laugh. Nope, probably our family. No matter, I'm ready to take that step in my life.

Minutes turn to hours before Kate calls me back with an update. "I really hate that you make me do this, you know?"

"Liar, you love it."

"You're right. Okay, Adi posted last night that she typed "the end." First, I hate that I can't even fucking read this book because now I'll always envision your sorry ass as the hero, and my eyes will have to be bleached if there's a sex scene. So, thanks for that."

"You're welcome. Continue," I say, leaning back

in my desk chair, feet propped on the desk with my ankles crossed.

"Well, she finished her manuscript. Actually, hold on . . ." I hear a click here and there in the background and then a snort. "She's a sneaky one. She posted her word count last week and then again last night with the post she finished. It's the same number. She finished this book a week ago but only told us last night. I wonder why she did that?"

"What else?" I ask, skirting right past her monologue, I don't care when she finished it, only what she's going to do now.

"That's it. There's nothing else. But, that's not uncommon. So many authors burn the midnight oil and push themselves. It's likely she hasn't had a hot meal or a shower in a week. She could sleep for the next three days and not even realize it."

Sighing, I stand from the chair and walk to the kitchen for something to drink. Glancing at the clock I looked at this morning, I note it's closer to dinner time than lunch.

"Spence?"

"Yeah?"

"Why don't you call her? I mean, you obviously care about what she's up to and how she is. The time you spent together, it sounds like more than friendship or colleagues."

It was. I can't tell my sister that though. How do I explain the level of my feelings to her when I've barely scratched the surface with Aggi herself? Sure, I told her we became friends. I relayed stories of our stops across the country, the crazy fans, and everything the public already knows about. I kept the intimate and real moments we shared between us. Our time here in my home, our nights making love, and the day at the Hall of Fame. Those moments are ours and ours alone, something I'm holding close to the vest until I can talk to Aggi.

"Maybe I'll call her this weekend."

Scoffing, Kate accuses me of being a liar and then begins catching me up on the kids and what everyone is up to. She may have wanted to sell them this morning but now she can't stop sharing their milestones.

A bell rings through the house. The front gate.

"Kate, I have to go. Someone's at the gate. I'll look at my calendar and plan a visit soon, okay?"

"Okay, bye baby bro."

Ending the call, I push the call button for the gate as I switch the screen on to see who is there.

"May I help you?" I ask into the microphone as a man leans out the window of a van with writing on the side.

"I'm with Rapid Delivery Services and have a delivery for Spencer Garrison."

Freddy mentioned he'd be sending a few boxes of stuff I have to sign for a charity auction, so I buzz the guy through. I swear if one of the items in these boxes is a life-size cutout of me again, I'm sending Freddy an ant farm. Minus the farm.

Outside I hear a car door close followed immediately by a second door before there are footsteps on the porch. Before the delivery guy can knock, I open the door and the person before me surprises me.

Aggi.

Damn she's a sight for sore eyes. The vision before me is the perfect combination of Agnes Sylvester and Adeline Snow. Her long hair is down in soft waves falling across her shoulders where she's sporting a light pink sweater covering a T-shirt that says something about being a book nerd. A pair of form-fitting jeans clad her amazing legs while a pair of black and white Chucks finish her look. She's nerdy chic and absolutely perfect.

"Hi." Her voice is quiet as a slight smile graces her face. I start to respond but notice a box in her hand.

"What are you doing here?"

"Delivering a package?" It's a question not a statement although she's holding a package and there's a delivery man standing behind her. "If you want me to go, I will but I need to let Charlie know so he can finish his route." I look behind her to the man I assume is Charlie. He's standing far enough back to give us privacy, but the way he's shifting I can tell he's ready to run.

"I don't want you to go, Aggi. Charlie?" The man nods. "I've got this. Thanks for the delivery." My gaze drops to my girl and I wink as a blush creeps across her cheeks.

We stand staring at each other as Charlie hops in

his van and pulls away. A few seconds tick by and then Aggi clears her throat, pulling me from my thoughts. Or my staring is more like it.

"Oh, shit. Sorry. Come in. Let me take this for you," I offer as I take the box from her hands and step aside to let her in the house. She tentatively steps forward, and I allow myself a quick glance down her body as she does.

"Can I get you something to drink? A glass of wine or water?"

"No, no thank you. I didn't think this through. I guess I'm kind of stuck here now." She pulls her finger between her teeth nervously. "Do you think a ride share will come all the way out here? Is there a taxi service in town? I'm staying at the little Bed 'n' Breakfast in town."

"Let's worry about that later." Nodding, a look of relief crosses her face, and I smile as I place the box on the table and take her hand in mine, pulling her to me. I could do more small talk or ask her what she's doing here in Lexington, but I don't. She's here. She came to me. That's all I want to focus on now.

She lands against me with an oomph as I cup her cheeks with my hands and lean down to kiss her. My lips are light as they brush hers, a test to see how she responds. Her grip on my forearms is strong and I take that as an invitation to increase our kiss. Licking the crease of her lips, I beg her to open with my movements and she rewards me quickly. The moment our tongues meet, it's hotter than the warmest Texas summer day. Her breaths are fast and match my own as our kiss deepens. Bending, I pick her up and wrap her legs around my hips as I walk us to the couch.

She lets me devour her mouth and pull her closer to me. Chest to chest, our hearts beat in tandem and I need more. Before I can make a move, Aggi pulls back, breaths labored and cheeks flushed, she looks drunk. Drunk on me. On us.

"I . . . I brought you something."

Chuckling, I place my hand to the back of her head and pull her lips to mine again but after a quick peck, she pulls back again.

"Please, Spencer. I need—"

She doesn't finish her statement and instead hops off my lap, almost kneeing me in the balls before she gasps, and I smile and wave her off. Some things don't change. Whispering "Sorry," she scampers off to retrieve the box on the table.

"I need you to open this."

Shifting myself on the couch, finding some relief from the wood I'm sporting, I take the box from her hands and tap the spot next to me on the couch. Climbing on the couch to the space next to me, she kneels and watches intently as I open the box. Tossing the lid aside, I look down at a . . . binder? She brought me a binder.

"A binder?"

Smiling, she says, "Open it."

Flipping the binder open, I look down at the first page.

Switch Stance

A Sports Romance

By Agnes Sylvester

"What is this?"

"It's our story. Well, it's my perspective of us. Of our time together and how I feel. About you. About us. That title seemed sort of perfect." She clears her throat and pushes a lock of hair behind her ear. "Since, you know my natural instinct is to run away from intense feeling, and this time I had to change directions to get where I wanted. Maybe they'll change the title, or something, I don't know . . ."

Her words peter out as I look back down at the binder and start flipping the pages. Page after page are words upon words. It's her book. Her book is about us.

"I don't understand." I sound like a moron because it's clear she wrote a book. A book about us.

"I freaked, Spencer. I have lived in my head for so long with you as my fantasy. You were always this unattainable celebrity and, in most cases, an inspiration for the characters I wrote. I won't go into details on how you inspired some of my most beloved male characters, but you did. Then you came into my life for real, and it was more than I could have imagined. You didn't think I was a complete idiot or embarrassment. You saw the real me and you didn't dismiss me. I had all these feelings I couldn't process. How much of what I was feeling was the version of you I had made up in my head, in my characters, and how much was real? Then the muse thing happened, and I was mortified. I assumed I'd been betrayed by a friend and that everyone in the world, or the book world at least, would know what a complete fraud I was."

"Sweetheart, you are not a fraud. How many times do I have to tell you that?"

"I know. I mean, I don't *know,* but I'm trying. Regardless, it's how I was feeling. And I freaked out. I was in my own head, and I refused to hear what you were saying. I'd been blocked for so long and I was doubting my ability as a writer on top of everything else."

"And this?" I ask, pointing to the binder.

"I got out of my own way. I let myself believe it all, and the writing fog came. I wrote and wrote until my fingers cramped. I dictated when I couldn't type another word. I put everything I felt, that you'd said to me. I put it all to paper and the result is this."

"It says Agnes Sylvester."

"That's for you. The final draft submitted to my editor says Adeline Snow. But for you, I wanted you to have this from me. The real me. The one you see. The one I am when I'm with you. I'm sorry I ran. I'm sorry I didn't believe you."

Tossing the binder aside, I pull Aggi back into my lap and kiss her with all that I am, all that we are, and all that I know we'll be. Pulling back, looking at my girl, I smile. "You owe me a lot of nights, baby."

A shy smile is my response, and I take it as an invitation as I stand and put her over my shoulder in a fireman's hold. We make it three steps down the hall to my room when she kicks the wall and knocks a picture off the wall.

"Dammit."

Laughing, I smack her ass as I cross the threshold to my room and my bed.

Epilogue

Aggi

1 year later

"**A**re you sure I look okay?"

I glance anxiously in the mirror, smoothing down my dress and turning this way and that. I bought this green halter dress just for tonight. It makes me feel like one of the pink ladies in *Grease*. Except green. But the effect is still the same. Adeline Snow is out in full force and she looks fierce. I think.

Honestly, I don't know. Maybe she looks like a clown. This is the brightest red I've worn on my lips in a while.

Spencer wraps his arms around my waist from behind and kisses me on the neck, right on the spot that always makes me relax. It usually makes me horny as well, but not today. Today I'm too amped up.

"You look amazing, Aggi. Like any man's wet dream." I cringe because, ew. That sounds messy. "Now let's get a move on," he continues with a slap to my ass, making me squeak. "The driver's waiting and we can't afford to be late today."

Walking quickly, but not so fast that I stumble in my peep toe heels, I grab my black clutch and we make our way out the door. Spencer has pulled out all the stops today with a black Lincoln Town Car and driver to match. He holds the door open for me and I'm grateful because it means Spencer has both hands free to ensure I get into the car safely.

I don't know why I'm so nervous. It's not like it's my big day.

Once we're situated comfortably and the driver has pulled out into the road, I retrieve my new smart phone from my clutch to check my emails.

Yes, I said smart phone. Spencer finally convinced me to ditch my beloved flip phone when we moved to LA, mostly because of the GPS. Nothing would surprise us less than if I got lost in Los Angeles and ended up in Compton overnight.

Plus, I need to be able to check my emails a few times a day to make sure contract negotiations are going well. *Switch Stance* ended up being my most popular book to date, hanging out in the number one spot of the New York Times Best Seller list for twelve weeks. Very quickly, the movie rights were sold to a big production company and a screenplay is in the process of being adapted.

Who knew that the one book I resisted writing for so long is the one book that resonated with people so much? I never would have guessed so many people have as many insecurities as I do. But I suppose that's what happens when you can't get out of your own head long enough to notice that what others present is not always what they really feel. You have to dig a little deeper for that information.

Hence, why we are temporarily located in Los Angeles. Until the movie is either wrapped or scrapped, this is where we are based. The rest of the time we spend at his home in Lexington. I like it there. He was right; it's quiet and peaceful and calming for my brain. It's helped me get my flow back. I still write about extreme sports, but a lot of my stories are about what happens in the off-season when the athletes aren't surrounded by teammates and not the competition aspect. It's a big change, but the readers have embraced it so far.

Pulling up the internet, I see no new emails, thank goodness because I can hardly think straight right now. But there are quite a few text notifications, including from the moms.

Jan: I can't wait to see pictures of tonight. It's like you're living in one of your books. SWOON! Love you.

Mom: Your rank has risen by 14.2% today. Clearly the anticipation of tonight's ceremony is having a positive marketing affect. Well done. I love you. Love, Mom.

I smirk. While I'm getting used to using a smart phone, my mother is just now learning the appropriate way to text. Must be a family trait.

Donna, on the other hand, is just trying to keep herself calm. All three of her texts are full of shouty capitals.

Donna: OHMYGOD I JUST LISTENED TO YOUR NEW AUDIOBOOK!!

Donna: WHO IS THIS NARRATOR AND WHERE DID YOU FIND HIM???

Donna: I NEED HIM!!! PLEASE, PLEASE, PLEASE HOOK ME UP WITH HAWK WEAVER FOR MY NEXT BOOK! AND MAYBE FOR MY BED!!

I snort a laugh and show the texts to Spencer, who also snorts a laugh. What Donna doesn't know, and I'll never tell, is "Hawk Weaver" is my own dear best friend, Todd. Yes, the same Todd that was too small to play any team sports in high school and can't nail a British accent to save his life is being lusted over by the glamorous Donna Moreno because of his deep, sexy voice. He's going to get a kick out of that. And possibly strut around like a peacock for the foreseeable future.

Her excitement shouldn't surprise me, though. Multiple times I've seen his name on "Top Narrator" lists, and he's only completed the one project so far. If Donna's response is any indication, I'll have more people messaging me about how they can contact the man behind the sexy voice, so maybe it's a good thing he decided to create a persona.

Once Todd finished voicing that first book, he came up with the grand idea that he needed a pseudonym "to keep the ladies from getting too close." His words, not mine. So he chose to combine the names of his two favorite skaters, Tony Hawk and Gregg Weaver into the perfect persona for his new career. Spencer got a kick out of that.

Me: Remind me when I get home and I'll send you his contact info. I have to look it up.

Donna: Oh! I forgot about today! Have fun and tell Spencer I said good luck!

Tossing my phone back in my clutch, I reach over and grab Spencer's hand.

"You nervous?"

He drags his gaze from the window and turns to smile at me. He looks calm on the outside, but I know him, and his confidence is waning a bit. "A little. So many of the people I've admired are going to be there. It's all surreal, ya know?"

I squeeze his hand and smile back at him because I do know. Every day I get to spend with the man of my dreams feels the same way. "You deserve this, babe. I'm so proud of you."

Leaning in, he gives me a soft kiss on the lips, only pulling back when we feel the car come to a stop, allowing me an opportunity to wipe the red lipstick off his face.

The door opens, and I look deep into his eyes. "You ready?"

He takes a spine-stealing breath and nods. "As ready as I'll ever be."

"Then let's do this."

Stepping out of the car first, my very hot boyfriend turns and extends his hand, helping me out and to my feet. We smile and wave to the crowd, the flash of cameras all around us, as we make our way to the front of the Skateboarding Hall of Fame.

•••

Spencer

As much as I prepared myself for tonight, I couldn't have known how overwhelming it all would be. The ridiculous red carpet, the interviews, and the number of handshakes I've had to endure is something I assumed only Hollywood actors had to deal with. I'm just some kid who happened to be good in a halfpipe and made a career out of a sport I love. Now, as I look around the room filled with men and women I have admired most of my life, the only person I want to find is my girl.

The last year with Aggi has been a roller coaster. After she showed up at my house with her manuscript of our love story, we spent a few days holed up in my house in Lexington before her phone started ringing off the hook. Finally, I set her up in my office with her laptop and more coffee than I'd ever seen a person drink. She worked her way through her edits and rewrites before submitting her final draft to the publisher. From that moment on, it was chaos. The book blew up and our relationship was front and center. Everyone had a slight glimpse into our life.

Both of our careers took off. My foundation received more and more recognition for the work we were doing with the skate parks and rec centers, but it was the new outreach for children with special needs that put us on the map. Celebrities, athletes from all over, and even politicians wanted to get involved. It's been overwhelming, and yet it justified and confirmed my choice to retire was the right one. Then, about three months ago, the invitation for tonight came.

Induction in the Skateboarding Hall of Fame. My ultimate childhood goal reached. Tonight, as I accept the honor, the girl of my dreams is with me to share the moment. It's possible she's more excited about this night than I am. I foresee a little bit of fangirling on her part as she meets more skateboarding royalty.

Of course, Kate is here and driving me crazy. The day after Aggi appeared at my house with her manuscript, I called Kate and called off the private detective work she was doing. Her rant about giving up on what could be and my happy ending was cut short when I surprised her with Aggi on the screen. Her squeal damn near blew out my eardrums, but it was worth it to show her I had in fact found my happy ending. One of the greatest moments of the last year, though, was the day Aggi and I visited Kate and her family and Aggi confessed her true identity as they shared a bottle of wine. Her mind was blown, and it was spectacular.

I tap the small velvet box in my jacket pocket. I've been carrying this around with me for weeks. Waiting for the right time to pop the question. There's no doubt in my mind that Aggi and I are forever, and this ring is the final piece we need to make it official. Mostly for everyone else. We know who we are.

Still scouring the room, a group of people disburse a few feet away, and like a vision from the heavens, my girl appears. I swear she gets more beautiful each and every day. As she learns to believe in herself and see herself through my eyes, she blossoms. I've always been proud of her, but the way she's embraced the craziness of the last year I stand in awe of her.

Her eyes find mine and a sweet smile greets me. I take a few steps toward her, maybe this is the moment I've waited for. Just as I touch the box through my jacket, a hand grabs my forearm.

"Mr. Garrison, it's time."

Shit. Another missed opportunity. I look up at Aggi who smiles and waves me off. It's time for my induction. I follow the woman to the stage as she begins gesturing for everyone to take their spots. Aggi, moves her way to the front and whispers "I love you" at the exact moment I think I may hurl from nerves. Saying those three words back to her, I take a deep breath and wait for my turn to speak.

Taking my place at the podium, I look around the room before speaking.

"I still cannot believe I'm here. Some days I feel like I'm still a five-year-old kid on Christmas morning. That Santa sure was a sucky board buyer." The crowd laughs and I look at Aggi who is probably wanting to tell me "I told you so" since she suggested the small joke at poor Santa's expense. "I never dreamed that morning I opened my first board that it would all lead to this moment. The last twenty-five years of my life have been a whirlwind. I've traveled the world, met some of my idols, many are in this room tonight, and suffered injuries I wasn't sure I'd recover from. Above it all, I've been given opportunities. Not only opportunities to see and participate in amazing events but to give back. Without this sport and this career, I wouldn't be able to give back through The Garrison

Foundation."

Clearing my throat, I find my girl in the audience. Her eyes are glassy, and her smile is wide. Speaking only to her, I continue. "I never believed in fate and destiny but then last year something amazing happened. I went on a getaway with my sister and met a woman who threw my boring black and white world into a sea of color. I began to see life and the world through different eyes, and because of her I'm a better man. To the world, she is Adeline Snow, New York Times Bestselling Author. To me, she'll always be the sunshine in my days and the inspiration for my tomorrows. I love you, baby. Thank you for believing in me."

The applause is deafening as I look down at the woman I love. Gone is the armor of a persona she used to hide behind. Sure, to the world she's still Adeline Snow. They can have that version of her. I'll take Agnes Sylvester, the quirky, talented, beautiful, and caring woman who will be my wife and share my life forever.

Not all happy endings are written, some are lived.

Acknowledgements

As with any book, there are a ton of people to thank. We could thank each other, but one of us would be uncomfortable and the other one would cry. It's up you to decide which is which. And frankly, it depends on our old ass hormones and who has been drinking. So we're gonna skip that part and get to the good stuff.

Kiersten Hill, Megan Addison, Marisol Scott and Kate Spitzer for keeping our secret locked up tight and giving us the first round of feedback. Spencer and Aggi thank you for that.

An extra special shout out to Megan and Kate – Megan for all the phenomenal graphics and Kate for being in the car and helping us brainstorm while we road tripped through Texas. However, you get points off for not telling us there was fudge because you were too engaged in the story line.

Alyssa Garcia from Uplifting Designs for knocking this cover out of the skate park. You didn't just deal with one crazy this time. You dealt with two! And you did it with grace.

Our editor Karen Lawson for double checking how to do the elipses. Who knew there were so many options? And by the way, thank you for checking our words and making sure they weren't just the two of us sharing inside jokes.

Amelié Vahle for using those eagle eyes to make

sure we didn't miss anything. Hope we sparked some flashbacks and brought up some good memories with the husband!

M.E. Carter's mom for reading through and finding last minute mistakes BEFORE it got published this time. (I should have done that with the last 10 books. Lesson learned.)

Andrea Johnston's husband for answering questions about old school skateboarding and punk rock music. Who knew that trivia would come in handy someday?

One more thing…. Alyssa Garcia didn't just design the cover. She supported our commitment to donate money to charity so much that she donated her formatting services. DONATED! For that, we can never thank you enough.

Lastly… readers, bloggers, authors, friends, we tip our skateboards to you for all the love we've received with this project. Our whole goal was to use what we know to give back to our communities. But that would have been in vain if it weren't for all of you and your excitement. We're thrilled to be a part of a community that wants to work for the greater good right along with us. We love you.

About the Authors

M.E. Carter and Andrea Johnston are romance writers who have come together to bring you a fun sports romantic comedy! Combining their sense of humor, beliefs in love, and sarcasm, this writing duo has crossed over two of their most popular series - the #MyNewLife and Country Road Series with the sole purpose of bringing laughter and love to their readers while tapping into their charitable hearts.

Find Andrea Johnston on...

Website
www.andreajohnstonauthor.com

Facebook
www.facebook.com/AndreaJohnstonAuthor

Instagram
www.instagram.com/andrea_johnston15

Find M.E. Carter on...

Website
www.authormecarter.com

Facebook
www.facebook.com/authorMECarter

Instagram
www.instagram.com/authormecarter

Other Books by M.E. Carter

Hart Series
Change of Hart
Hart to Heart
Matters of the Hart

Texas Mutiny Series
Juked
Groupie
Goalie
Megged

#MyNewLife Series
Getting a Grip
Balance Check
Pride & Joie
Amazing Grayson